THE MUMMY'S REVENGE

Other Apple Paperbacks
you will enjoy:

The Book of the Banshee
Anne Fine

The Fortuneteller in 5B
Jane Breskin Zalben

Tales from Academy Street
Martha Derman

The Ghost in the Noonday Sun
Sid Fleischman

THE MUMMY'S REVENGE

Original title: *The Mummy Monster Game*

ROY POND

AN
APPLE
PAPERBACK

SCHOLASTIC INC.
New York Toronto London Auckland Sydney

For Brenda, my helper,
who first encouraged me to write
for young readers

If you purchased this book without a cover, you should be aware that this book is stolen property. It was reported as "unsold and destroyed" to the publisher, and neither the author nor the publisher has received any payment for this "stripped book."

No part of this publication may be reproduced in whole or in part, or stored in a retrieval system, or transmitted in any form or by any means, electronic, mechanical, photocopying, recording, or otherwise, without written permission of the publisher. For information regarding permission, write to Omnibus Books, part of the Ashton Scholastic Group, 52 Fullarton Road, Norwood, South Australia 5067.

ISBN 0-590-48374-9

Copyright © 1993 by Roy Pond. All rights reserved. Published by Scholastic Inc., 555 Broadway, New York, NY 10012, by arrangement with Omnibus Books, part of the Ashton Scholastic Group. APPLE PAPERBACKS is a registered trademark of Scholastic Inc.

12 11 10 9 8 7 6 5 4 3   5 6 7 8 9/9

Printed in the U.S.A.   40

First Scholastic printing, October 1994

Contents

1

Playing in the Dark

Their cousin Harry held up a computer game box.

"This may be scary," he said in a warning voice. "Very scary. Are you ready to play the Mummy Monster Game?" He had promised to show them something special.

Josh and Amy looked at the cover. It showed a gruesome illustration of an Egyptian mummy wrapped in trailing bandages. Beneath it was written: "Your adventure quest is to enter the tomb of King Osiris and restore the king to life. But first you must find and gather together the lost and scattered pieces of his mummy. They are hidden in chambers guarded by underworld creatures who will set you challenges." Around the edges of the box were pictures of Egyptian gods—creatures with human bodies and the heads of birds, jackals, snakes and crocodiles.

They were sitting in Josh's bedroom: Josh, his sister Amy, and Harry, their ten-year-old cousin. Harry was staying with them while his mother was away in Egypt on an archaeological trip.

Josh was intrigued by the look of the game, although

he couldn't help thinking that the Egyptians must have been primitive to believe in such dumb-looking creatures. He supposed people were pretty ignorant thousands of years ago.

Amy was not impressed. She shook her head, making her brown pony-tail swing. "Sorry, no computer games." She turned to Josh with an accusing stare. "You know it's my turn to have the computer. You're just trying to hang on to it longer so you can play silly games. I've got to write my drama project."

Amy was writing a play to be performed by her class, and Josh had promised to set up the computer in her bedroom.

Josh shrugged. "I didn't know Harry had this game. You can have the computer later, Amy. Let's all have a play first."

"I'm not playing computer games."

"Please, you must," Harry said. "We must all play this game."

"Computer games are a waste of time." Amy looked despairingly around her twelve-year-old brother's bedroom. "Look at this place. It's like a computer game store in here." The shelves were stacked with game boxes and manuals. There were even games piled on top of the desk where Josh was supposed to sit and do his homework. "Once Josh gets his head stuck into a new game, there's no getting him out of it."

Sometimes Amy sounded like their mother, Josh thought, even though she was a year younger than he was. She didn't approve of his craze for computer games, and thought he should spend more of his time doing schoolwork. Amy felt a drive to achieve, like their mother, who worked as an advertising executive.

"There's no harm in a bit of fantasy," Josh said, defensively. "It's good for the imagination."

"But you always get so sucked into games! Your bedroom could be on fire and you wouldn't notice. Just think what you could do if you put some of that concentration into your schoolwork. You wouldn't get into nearly so much trouble, especially from Mum. She said you were to stop playing computer games and do some homework."

"Later."

Harry read from the back of the box, squinting at the fine print. "This game is really special. 'Be warned: the longer you take to complete the quest, the more mummy monsters will be set loose to challenge you. They have the power to destroy.' And here are some rules of the game. Listen! You can stop for breaks, and even turn off the game, but only after completing a challenge, and not in the middle of the action. The game has a special memory, so it will take you back to the stage you have reached."

"Let's play," Josh said, his eyes shining hungrily. "Give the disk to me and I'll load it up."

"I'm going," Amy said. "I think I'll do some homework."

"No," Harry said. "You've got to see this game. It's come all the way from Egypt. There's a little games shop in Cairo that sends me ancient Egyptian adventure games." Harry's parents travelled all over the world and Harry often went with them. His father was a university professor in ancient history and his mother, Josh and Amy's Aunt Jillian, was an Egyptologist. Harry had been to Egypt with her on several digs and he knew all about mummies and pyramids and pharaohs. He loved to brag about his experiences. "Please, Amy. We'll need all the help we can get."

"Why?"

"These Egyptian games are tricky. They need heaps of brain power."

Harry looked determined, Josh thought. He seemed eager for Amy to stay. Why would they need Amy to help them? She hardly knew a thing about computer games.

Amy balanced on the edge of a decision. Harry nodded hopefully, encouraging her to nod in agreement, but Amy wasn't giving in.

A visitor arrived to tip things Harry's way. A cat came in like a puff of ginger smoke, brushing himself in a furry greeting against Amy's leg.

"Hello, Spy," she said, bending to stroke his head. Spy was Amy's cat. He had been given his name because as a kitten he loved to spy on the family and used to creep after them to watch what they were doing.

Spy sprang on to the edge of Josh's bed and sat, head erect, neat and composed, regarding the computer screen with yellow eyes. He looked elegant and a bit Egyptian, like a carving of a cat Josh had seen in one of his history books.

"Spy's come to stay," Josh told Amy. "So you'd better say yes."

Amy shrugged. "All right, I'll stay, but only for a while. I know you, Josh. You'll spend days on a new game if you're given half a chance. One condition, though. You've got to stop when I say so."

Harry opened the game box and gave the computer disk to Josh. While Josh booted it up and the disk drive churned softly, Harry closed the curtains. Harry went to a private school, and he had broken up early for school holidays. Clearly he was going to have no trouble making himself at home while his cousins continued at school.

"Do we have to sit in the dark?" Amy said. "It's such a brilliant day."

"We need the right effect," Harry said firmly.

They sat down in front of the computer and started to play.

Weird Egyptian music—a flute, drums and a shimmering rattle sound—floated out of the monitor.

A group of three adventurers, representing the three players, appeared on the screen. They were dressed in khaki field clothes.

The figures approached the entrance to a tomb.

Josh swallowed. He knew it wasn't real, that it was only a computer game they were playing, but even so he felt tremors of nervous excitement. He glanced down at the empty game box, which was sitting on the desk in front of the monitor. The glow from the screen flared on the cover, and the picture of the mummy seemed to stir.

The three characters on the screen toiled up a cliff path high above the desert floor. The tomb entrance showed up as a narrow vertical shadow slanting into the cliff.

"It looks like the slot of our letterbox," Amy remarked.

"It may look like a letterbox," Harry said, showing off his knowledge, "but it wasn't used for posting letters. The ancient Egyptians posted a parcel in there, all wrapped up in hundreds of metres of linen and stamped with hieroglyphics addressed to the underworld—a mummy."

A panel with writing on it appeared on the screen. Amy read the words:

> THIS IS THE TOMB OF KING OSIRIS. HERE YOU WILL BEGIN YOUR QUEST TO FIND THE PIECES OF HIS MUMMY. YOU MUST PASS THROUGH THE DOORWAY INTO THE SILENCE OF THE TOMB.

Just then the bedroom door behind them creaked and opened. Light fell into the room, and the moving shadow of the door swept over the players at the computer.

Josh felt the shadow pass over him like a chill. He twisted round in his chair. Why had the door opened? Spy was still there, sitting on the bed. Maybe their mother's poodle, Tina, had bumped the door and poked her nose inside. But there was no sign of the dog now.

Josh felt a prickliness under his shirt, a feeling not entirely caused by the heat and stuffiness of his bedroom. The music playing on the monitor made the hairs stand up on his arms.

Harry went to the door and closed it again.

Josh sharpened his attention.

2

The Mummy Monster Game

"It's as black as a cave in here," Amy said. "Can we have a light on, please?"

Harry shook his head. "You've got to have the effect of a tomb to play this game. You're not scared of the dark, are you?"

"Scared of the dark?" Josh said scornfully. "Don't be dumb. This is my bedroom."

"You're right," Amy said, relaxing a bit. "We'll just pretend we're at the movies."

"Yes, but there's a mummy monster movie showing at this cinema," Harry said. He gave a deep growl.

Amy laughed. "Stop teasing, Harry!"

Josh decided that Harry was a bit of a ˌest. He was the sort of kid who was afraid of nothing, and who'd do anything to show off. He'd been busting to impress Josh and Amy ever since he'd arrived the night before, and he'd be with them for another fortnight before Aunt Jillian returned from Egypt.

If he wants to play games, I'll show him, Josh thought. He'd soon sort this kid out. Josh never knew what to think about other people or how to deal with them until he'd competed against them, or, better still, beaten them in a game. Games, especially computer games, had a way of sorting things out quickly. It was a sure way to prove who was best, beyond argument, bluff and bragging.

The music faded as the three little adventurers on the screen—two boys and a girl—reached the entrance to the tomb. One of the figures was smaller than the others.

Harry had the computer joystick in his hand. "Let's go inside," he said. "*I'm* not scared of tombs. I've been inside real ones."

"Aren't you afraid of anything, Harry?" Amy asked.

Harry beamed. "What's there to be scared of?"

Show off, Josh thought.

"Would you walk inside a real tomb, Josh?" Harry said, turning to his older cousin.

Harry was the sort of kid Josh felt he had to impress. The blue eyes seemed to expect big things of him. "Of course I would," he said, frowning.

Harry smiled in the glow from the computer screen. "Good. There's no need to be afraid of them, you know. Ancient Egyptian tombs weren't really graves. My mother told me. They were eternity machines—designed to carry the dead into eternity to meet the gods and to join the stars. They're not scary places at all. The walls are covered with brilliant pictures. The people in them look alive."

That made Egyptian tombs sound even creepier, Josh decided. He didn't like the idea of pictures looking alive in a tomb, even in a computer game.

Josh and Amy had been looking forward to having

Harry to stay so they could find out all about Aunt Jillian's discoveries in Egypt. Josh was learning about ancient Egypt in history at school. He had been keen to play Harry's mysterious Egyptian game, too. But now that they were playing it, he had a bad feeling. The idea of entering the realistically illustrated tomb sent an unexpected shiver through him.

Harry moved the joystick to choose the next move. He placed the cursor, a tiny arrow on the screen, against the tomb passage and clicked.

The graphics changed. Suddenly the explorers moved inside the deeper shadow of the tomb entrance. Josh had the feeling that the room itself had darkened and he had really stepped into a recess. As his eyes adjusted to the shadows, he saw that the way to the tomb was blocked by a barred iron gate with a lock on it. The tomb passage behind the bars looked darker than the inside of a cinema.

Harry moved the joystick. "Follow me and I'll show you to your sarcophagus," he joked, like an usher showing them to their seats at the movies.

Amy chuckled nervously. "Sarcophagus. That's a mummy coffin, isn't it?"

"That's right. The big ones, made of stone. They had smaller coffins inside them, usually made of wood or gold. You see, I know all about Egyptology."

A figure wearing an Arab head-dress and a *galabea* robe appeared abruptly out of the shadows. He drew a sword in a flashing movement.

Amy gasped. Josh jumped. It seemed as if the guard had actually stepped out in front of them, barring their way. It was like a 3-D effect or a hologram, Josh thought. He felt he could reach out and touch the challenger.

"Sorry, I should have expected it," Harry told them. "There's a guard on duty at the gate of the tomb. Most of the tombs in Egypt are guarded."

"Why do they have a guard outside? Is it to stop anyone trying to steal the treasures of Osiris?" Amy said.

The silence tingled.

"Maybe it's to try to stop the underworld monsters from coming out," Harry said.

Another panel jumped on to the screen. Harry read the words aloud:

> I AM MAHMOUD, THE TOMB GUARD. BEFORE YOU MAY ENTER THE SECRET TOMB OF OSIRIS, YOU MUST GIVE THE PASSWORD. WHO WAS THE WIFE OF OSIRIS?

"That's easy. The wife of Osiris was the goddess Isis." Harry typed in the name.

"I knew that," said Amy.

The tomb guard sheathed his sword and bowed. He took some keys from his robe, chose one, rattled it around in the keyhole and swung the gate open. The graphics on the screen were brilliant, with the colour and clarity of a movie. The gate gave a mournful iron sigh on its hinges. The sound was realistic too.

They went into the tomb passage.

Something happened then that shouldn't have happened. Josh felt a change in temperature on his skin as if he had passed out of the stuffiness of the bedroom and into an atmosphere of coldly sweating stone. The straight walls of the passage ran endlessly ahead, and the glowing perspective lines made by the corners of its floor and roof converged in the distance like railway lines. These lines seemed to be moving, pulsing towards the centre of the screen, drawing his eyes hypnotically to the point where they met. Josh felt a tug on his body, as if he were being dragged from his chair.

Lights appeared in the passage. Moving torches. Three yellow, probing beams opened up the darkness: two big, one small. It was as if the torches were being carried by the players.

"Why do I feel like this?" Amy said. "As if I'm being pulled along."

"The game is dragging us inside," Harry said in a spooky voice.

From Harry's direction, someone sprayed a wavy beam of torchlight over the tomb passage, like a vandal with a spraycan of paint.

Amy giggled. Josh had that bad feeling again. He moved his chair closer to his sister's. Then Amy grabbed his arm, making him jump. "We must stick together, Josh. You're not scared of computer games, are you?"

"I think he's a bit scared of this one," Harry said perceptively.

Josh glared at him in the dark. It wasn't going to be much fun playing with Harry. Josh felt enough responsibility being the oldest without having this kid trying to show him up all the time.

Harry manipulated the joystick. The torch beams

fanned over stone walls to reveal beautifully coloured paintings, scenes of people on the River Nile in strange boats—swept-up skiffs made of papyrus bundles. They were throwing what looked like boomerangs at wildfowl in a thicket of tall plants. The whites of their eyes were vivid and made their eyes throw dark, accusing stares.

"These graphics are amazing," Josh said. It felt as if they were actually moving along the stone-walled passageway, as if they were really part of the game.

"Shh," Amy said, putting her finger to her lips. "What's that sound?"

They listened. Far off they could hear the wailing of a woman in grief, a spirit-wrenching sound that trembled on the air.

Harry gave the stick a nudge.

The stone passageway led them to a doorway and an antechamber. To the right, an annexe ran off the antechamber. To the left, another doorway gave on to a burial chamber.

The wailing grew louder. A trickle of fear slid down the back of Josh's collar.

"Into the burial chamber," Harry said. "That's where it's coming from."

They moved into the chamber in response to directions from the joystick in Harry's fist. Their torch beams swished around, scouring the darkness.

The burial chamber was a large rectangular room with four square columns carved out of rock. Scenes from the Book of the Dead and the underworld journey of the soul crowded every centimetre of the walls. The ceiling was painted black, a night sky exploding with a golden galaxy of stars, gods and goddesses and creatures of ancient Egyptian mythology as well as sacred boats that carried the sun through the underworld by night and across the sky by day. Divinities stood in thronged ranks—some with heads of snakes, birds, crocodiles, dogs or apes; others wearing stars on their heads to indicate their status as stellar divinities. Bordering the figures were columns of small hieroglyphics written in white. They looked like a dusting of stars on the black sky of the ceiling.

Arched over all was the giant body of a woman.

"Look at that golden girl stretched across the ceiling," Amy said in admiration. "Who is she?"

"That's the sky goddess Nut," Harry told them.

An orange orb, the sun, wheeled through Nut's star-lined body, making its daily course through the heavens before emerging from her mouth. In a mirror image beside it, the same outstretched figure of Nut was shown swallowing the sun at night and allowing it to pass through her body to be reborn as the dawn.

The sounds of weeping and wailing still filled their ears. There was somebody in the tomb chamber.

The searching torches of the explorers found a stone sarcophagus in the centre of the chamber. The lid had been torn off it. Beside it, on the stone floor, knelt a young woman. She was bobbing up and down, clawing at the air with her fingernails and rending it with her cries of sorrow. There was dust in her hair and she wore torn blue clothes. Tears streamed down her face. It was a picture of a soul in deepest torment.

Another panel of writing appeared on the screen.

THIS IS ISIS. SHE WEEPS FOR THE MISSING MUMMY OF HER HUSBAND, KING OSIRIS. HIS MUMMY HAS BEEN ATTACKED BY HIS EVIL BROTHER SETH, THE EGYPTIAN DEVIL. IT HAS BEEN TORN INTO FRAGMENTS AND SCATTERED. YOU MUST HELP ISIS FIND THE FRAGMENTS AND PUT OSIRIS BACK TOGETHER SO THAT HE CAN COME TO LIFE AGAIN. THIS IS YOUR QUEST ... BUT HURRY. THE LONGER YOU TAKE TO COMPLETE THE QUEST, THE MORE MUMMY MONSTERS WILL BE SET LOOSE TO CHALLENGE YOU ...

"We must help Isis," Harry said. "We have to put the pharaoh together again. It's like a jigsaw puzzle with human parts. The legend of Osiris says that his fragments were scattered all over Egypt. The parts must be gathered before Osiris is resurrected so he can take his place as king and judge of the Egyptian underworld."

"He's going to be resurrected?" Amy said cautiously.

In answer to her question, another panel appeared on the screen.

IN EGYPTIAN MYTHOLOGY, OSIRIS WAS A MAN-GOD WHO SUFFERED AND DIED AND ROSE AGAIN TO REIGN ETERNALLY AS THE LORD OF THE AFTERWORLD AND THE JUDGE OF SOULS. HIS RISING FROM THE DEAD ASSURED EGYPTIANS OF ETERNAL LIFE, PROVIDED THEY COULD PROVE THAT THEY HAD LIVED GOOD LIVES.

"I don't follow that," Amy said to the screen. "That description sounds like Jesus. Surely it can't be right.

Osiris was a pagan god."

Another panel of words appeared:

> THE MYTH OF THE RESURRECTION OF OSIRIS WAS
> A PRE-ECHO OF AN EVENT THAT OCCURRED LATER
> IN HISTORY, THE RESURRECTION OF JESUS. THE
> FRAGMENTS OF THE MUMMY OF OSIRIS CAN BE
> FOUND AT THE ENDS OF SECRET PASSAGES IN
> SANCTUARIES GUARDED BY TOMB MONSTERS WHO
> ANSWER TO THE EVIL SETH'S BIDDING. THEY WILL
> POSE PROBLEMS FOR YOU TO SOLVE.

"Tell me about Seth," Amy said to Harry.

"He was the enemy of Osiris," Harry told her. "The Egyptians hated him so much for attacking the good King Osiris that his image and name were often hacked from ancient monuments. If you see him in the game, he will appear as a man with the shadow-head of a strange animal. The animal has square-tipped ears that stand up on his head and he has a drooping snout like an ant-eater or maybe a donkey or an okapi—nobody knows."

"Let's get on with the game," Josh said. "We've got to help Isis."

More instructions appeared on the screen. Harry read them out:

> TO BEGIN YOUR QUEST, YOU MUST FIND THE
> SECRET DOOR TO THE FIRST SANCTUARY. HERE IS
> YOUR CLUE: THE DOOR IS HIDDEN IN PHARAOH'S
> HOUSE OF ETERNITY. BUT BE QUICK. YOU ARE
> RUNNING OUT OF TIME.

"What's a house of eternity?" Amy asked.

"Not much of a clue, that's what," Harry said glumly. "You see, a house of eternity simply means a place that houses a mummy. This whole burial chamber is one. So we have no idea where to look. The doorway could be anywhere."

"I thought you knew about ancient Egypt," Josh said critically.

"Be fair," Amy said. "Harry hasn't played this game before."

"Even if I had, it might not help. Some of these games never play the same way twice."

3

The Locked Chamber

Harry spun the joystick, searching the burial chamber. The figure of Isis went on wailing, bobbing up and down.

"Let's get out of here," Amy said. "I can't bear the sound of that crying. It makes me want to cry too."

"Got any ideas?" Harry said.

Torchlight flashed around the chamber. As well as the lidless stone sarcophagus they saw pieces of tomb furniture, a black jackal statue, some ornamental chests, a leopard-headed couch with animal-shaped legs, an ostrich-feather fan, some swords, spears, bows and arrows, and a chariot.

"Where's all the gold and jewels?" Josh said. "I thought Egyptian tombs were stuffed with treasure."

"Hidden away," Harry said. "Or else robbed. Most tombs were robbed of treasure thousands of years ago. We must look carefully at all the pieces of tomb furniture remaining. One of them will take us to the secret passage."

"You mean it may give us a clue?" Amy said.

"Maybe. Or it may reveal a lever that opens a door. All we have to do is move the cursor arrow on the screen to the object and click. If it's hiding a clue, or a door, it will tell us."

"I don't like that jackal," Josh said. A black jackal crouched like a sphinx on a carrying pedestal. It had erect ears and a sharp snout. Its black eyes were outlined with gold paint, swept up at the corners.

Harry moved the cursor arrow over the image of the jackal and clicked. A box appeared.

> THIS IS ANUBIS, LORD OF THE MUMMY WRAPPINGS, INVENTOR OF THE MORTUARY RITES. HE LEADS THE DECEASED IN THE OTHER WORLD AND GUARDS THE TOMBS.

"That wasn't much help," Josh said.

"How about that casket?" Harry asked. "There could be something hidden in there." He moved the cursor and clicked.

> THIS IS AN ORNAMENTAL WOODEN COSMETICS BOX. INSIDE IT IS A MIRROR, A COMB, EYE MAKE-UP AND COSMETICS, PERFUMES AND UNGUENTS.

"Make-up! Not very interesting," Josh said.

"That's the wrong attitude," Amy said. "It might give us a clue. I want to see inside that make-up kit. Can you make it open, Harry?"

Obediently, Harry clicked twice.

The cosmetics box opened to reveal its contents: a bronze mirror, an ivory comb, spoons, silver tweezers, and a messy collection of jars, pots, palettes and brushes. It looked like the bottom of their mother's make-up drawer in her bedroom dresser.

"What's that little ivory duck?" Amy asked.

Harry hunted it down and clicked.

> THIS IS AN OINTMENT BOX IN THE FORM OF A
> DUCK. TO OPEN IT, SLIDE THE WINGS APART.

"Do it!" Amy said.

Harry clicked. The flat wings on the duck's back slid apart to reveal a creamy liquid.

"That's clever!" Amy said. "What's that palette with the brushes? It looks like eyeliner."

A panel with words appeared.

> ANCIENT EGYPTIAN WOMEN LOVED TO BEAUTIFY
> THEMSELVES WITH MAKE-UP. THEY ADORNED
> THEIR EYES WITH A DARK COSMETIC KNOWN
> TODAY AS KOHL. THE DARK "ALMOND-EYED"
> OUTLINE OF KOHL MADE THEIR EYES SEEM MYSTE-
> RIOUS AND ALLURING. IT ALSO PROTECTED THEIR
> EYES FROM THE SUN'S GLARE, AND HAD HEALING
> PROPERTIES THAT HELPED PREVENT EYE DISEASES.
> THAT'S WHY MEN WORE IT TOO.

"See, you might learn something, Josh," Amy said. "Can we have a close-up of that pretty hand-mirror? Your game's not so bad, Harry. It's a bit creepy, but it teaches us things."

That was a worry, Josh thought. If Amy liked it, it must be educational. "This isn't a trick to give us history lessons, is it, Harry?" he said suspiciously. "I want some excitement."

"You'll have excitement all right. Remember what the game told us? The longer we play, the more mummy monsters will be let loose. See that flashing light at the side of the screen? That means there's something coming to get us."

"Get us? What do you mean, 'get us'?" Amy said, the new enthusiasm draining from her voice.

"Look."

Harry clicked the arrow over a corner of the screen, which opened up to show a sort of map of underground passages, like an ants' nest.

"We're here," Harry said, pointing to a flashing square at the end of one passage. "That's the burial chamber. But look what's trying to find its way through the maze of passages to reach us."

They saw it now.

"Ooh, yuk! It's gross! What is it?" Amy said.

"A mummy monster."

Shuffling jerkily along a passage, its tattered arms outstretched, came a giant mummified figure with the head of a crocodile.

"But what happens if we can't get out of here? Can it get in?"

"Look at the size of it. It could just knock down a wall," Harry said. "We'd better concentrate, or that monster could destroy us."

"This is turning scary," Amy said.

"It's only a game," Harry said, taking the maze off the screen and returning them to the burial chamber.

"Listen to poor Isis. She doesn't think it's a game."

Had Harry raised the level of the sound? Suddenly the cries of Isis seemed to fill the room and ring in their ears.

"We'd better get out of here," Josh said.

4

The Mummy Monster

They felt a pounding under their chairs. What could it be? Was there a piledriver at work somewhere in their street? Or was it the thudding footsteps made by the mummy monster with the crocodile's head? Josh searched the screen for a clue, and his eyes settled on the lightweight chariot that stood in one corner. "Let's try the chariot," he suggested. "Give me the controls, quickly. Let me have a go."

"No, let Harry," Amy said anxiously.

"Don't you think I can do it?" Josh said, hurt. "I've played a lot more games than Harry."

"I know you're good at games, Josh. But Harry knows about Egyptian things."

"You only have a turn after you've solved a problem," Harry said firmly. "And the person who solves a problem gets first go at the next one—unless they want to hand over."

What a bossy kid, Josh thought. He shrugged. Oh well, I suppose it *is* his game. "But maybe the chariot's a clue," he persisted.

"I'll try it," Harry agreed. He clicked, producing an

information box.

HORSE-DRAWN WAR CHARIOTS WERE INTRO-
DUCED INTO THE NILE VALLEY IN AROUND 1600 BC.
EGYPTIAN INNOVATION MADE THEM LIGHTER AND
FASTER. THESE TWO-WHEELER VEHICLES WERE
MADE OF WOOD, LEATHER AND METAL, AND
DRAWN BY TWO SWIFT HORSES. THEY CARRIED
ONE OR, IN THIS CASE, TWO PASSENGERS, THE
CHARIOTEER AND THE PHARAOH, WHO USED IT
AS A PLATFORM FROM WHICH TO FIRE ARROWS AT
THE ENEMY. CHARIOTS WERE ALSO USED BY THE
PHARAOH ON JOURNEYS INTO THE DESERT TO
HUNT LIONS, USING BOWS AND ARROWS.

The box vanished.

They were looking at the burial chamber again. The
figure of Isis was still bobbing up and down. Her tears
were streaming to the floor of the chamber and disappearing down cracks in the stone.

Disappearing? That gave Josh an idea. Where were
the tears going? Maybe there was a hollow underneath
the passage. Maybe this was the way out.

"I think Isis is standing over a secret passage," he
said. "Look, her tears are going through the floor. There
must be a hollow underneath."

"Good thought," Amy said.

Harry moved the cursor to the figure of Isis and
clicked.

THIS IS ISIS. SHE WEEPS FOR THE MISSING MUMMY
OF HER HUSBAND, KING OSIRIS. HIS MUMMY HAS

BEEN ATTACKED BY HIS EVIL BROTHER SETH, THE
EGYPTIAN DEVIL. IT HAS BEEN TORN INTO FRAG-
MENTS AND SCATTERED. YOU MUST HELP ISIS FIND
THE FRAGMENTS AND PUT OSIRIS BACK TOGETHER
SO THAT HE CAN COME TO LIFE AGAIN. THIS IS
YOUR QUEST ...

"Not so clever. We've already had that information,"
Josh said, disappointed.

"I wonder how close the mummy monster is now,"
Harry said thoughtfully. "Shall we take a look?"

"No thanks." Amy shivered.

"Just a peek."

Harry moved the cursor arrow and punched the
keyboard, and again the computer printed the grid of
passages over the screen. They saw the mummy monster
rounding a corner. He had entered a passage that led
directly to the burial chamber.

Amy gave a squeal of alarm. "Now I know why I
don't like computer games. They're too scary. Do something! Can't we stop playing?"

"Only at the right time," Harry reminded her. "Not
when a mummy monster's about to burst through the
wall. We can only do it after passing a test."

"Well, let's hurry," Amy said urgently.

"What was the clue again?" Josh asked. His voice
came out sounding gruff and strained. His hands felt
damp, and his eyes were hurting from staring at the
screen.

A helpful box appeared.

REMEMBER YOUR CLUE: THE DOOR TO THE FIRST

23

SANCTUARY IS HIDDEN IN PHARAOH'S HOUSE OF
ETERNITY.

"I want to look at something," Amy said.

"Not the cosmetics again," Josh said edgily. "Not
now. Come on Harry. You call the shot." He was glad
now that he hadn't taken the controls.

"I have an idea," Amy persisted. "It was something
you told us, Harry. You said that a house of eternity
means simply a place that houses a mummy. Well, a
coffin houses a mummy, too, doesn't it?"

Harry whistled. "You've done it!" he said. "You're
exactly right. Coffins are houses of eternity too. Miniature tombs."

"Stop sounding like one of those boxes on the screen,"
Josh said irritably. "Do something."

Harry shook his head. "Not me." He handed the
joystick to Amy.

"I don't want it," Amy said, shrinking away.

"You've solved the riddle. You can take over."

"But we don't even know if I'm right. You keep it."

"No, you."

Josh made an impatient strangled sound. "While you
two are arguing, the mummy monster's breathing down
our necks."

"What do I do?" Amy said, taking the joystick from
Harry.

"Just put the cursor over the coffin and click."

Amy moved the cursor. The tiny arrow jumped like a
nervous grasshopper all over the screen.

"Put it on the coffin!" Josh told her.

24

"I'm trying, I'm trying!"

The cursor crawled over the screen to the coffin. Now there was a crashing sound. Something was banging on the stone wall of the chamber.

"It's old crocodile head!"

"Click, Amy!" Josh yelled.

Amy clicked.

A box appeared.

> YOU'RE ON THE RIGHT TRACK. COFFINS WERE ACTUALLY HOUSES OF ETERNITY TOO, THE MOST NECESSARY OF ALL TOMB ITEMS. THEY WERE MADE IN THE FORM OF MINIATURE TOMB BUILDINGS, SOMETIMES WITH PALACE FACADES AND FALSE DOORS, AND LIKE TOMBS THEY WERE DECORATED WITH MAGICAL TEXTS TO GUIDE THE SOUL THROUGH THE UNDERWORLD.

"That's what you just said, Harry," Josh said suspiciously. "Are you sure you haven't played this game before?"

"We're nearly there, but we haven't quite solved it yet. The door," Amy said. "Look, there's a false door on the side of the sarcophagus." She dragged the pointer jerkily across the screen towards the doorway carved into the stone, and clicked.

The mummy monster slammed against the wall. The chamber shook, and the darkness seemed to tremble. *But this is my bedroom*, Josh thought. *How can I be feeling this?* Pieces of the wall crashed to the floor. Amy ducked. Josh cowered.

But now there was another sound, the sound of stone

grating on stone.

"Move the joystick to take us to the sarcophagus," Harry instructed Amy. She shifted the stick and they were swept forward to a view over the edge of the sarcophagus. They peered over.

The bottom of the empty coffin had slid away, and the players now saw a flight of stairs running into the darkness.

5

The First Fragment

The mummy monster roared into the burial chamber, bellowing like a bull. It was a wild sight. It had the body of a giant mummy, and its scaly crocodile's head and jaws were bearded with broken bandages.

The three adventurers went over the edge of the stone sarcophagus to the flight of stairs. A shadow deeper than the gloom of the burial chamber fell over them as the monster made a dive at them.

"Quickly!" Harry shouted.

The players almost felt themselves being sucked down the stairs. There was a grating sound above their heads as the base of the sarcophagus closed again, sealing them from the monster.

"Whew!" Amy said. "Maybe it's time for that break."

"We haven't done anything yet," Josh said.

"Haven't done anything? That's gratitude, Josh. I've just saved you from a crocodile monster."

"Very clever, too, Amy," Harry said, making up to her.

"Thank you, Harry."

Josh looked up at the ceiling in the dark. Were these two going to hog the game all day? "We haven't even found the first piece of Osiris."

"Josh is right," Harry said. "We can't have a break until we've found the first piece. It'll be at the end of this passage."

"They said it would be guarded by a tomb monster. What's going to happen next?" Amy said.

As if to oblige, the box with words in it appeared on the screen.

THE MUMMY FRAGMENTS OF OSIRIS MUST BE FOUND IN A SPECIAL ORDER. FIRST ONE FOOT, THEN THE OTHER, THEN HIS LEGS IN TURN, HIS ARMS IN TURN, HIS HEAD, HIS FOUR ORGANS, HIS BODY, HIS EYE AND FINALLY, MOST IMPORTANT OF ALL, HIS HEART, IN THE SHAPE OF A JEWELLED SCARAB. THE FIRST FRAGMENT, HIS FOOT, LIES AT THE END OF THIS PASSAGE IN A SANCTUARY GUARDED BY A MONSTER DEMI-GOD WITH A SERPENT'S HEAD. HE WILL POSE A RIDDLE FOR YOU. IF YOU CAN SOLVE IT, YOU WILL GAIN THE FOOT OF OSIRIS.

"Yuk, a mummy's foot."

"Isis wants it, remember. Don't be scared—it's just a game," Harry told her.

"Yes, but it's a horror game."

"Well, just think of it as a horror movie," Harry said, giving another playful growl.

"The only real horror is you, Harry," Amy said good-naturedly, softening. "All right, let's go on. Down the passage we go. But I must say this game of yours is very spooky. It feels as if we're really in it."

She moved the joystick and they were swept along the length of the passage, their torches throwing cones of light on the floor and walls.

"Nothing horrible is going to jump out at us, is it?" Amy said. "I hope not." Her voice echoed eerily.

Strange, Josh thought. His bedroom didn't normally echo.

The passage widened and opened into a chamber. A dim fall of light from the high ceiling drew their eyes to a small pedestal beside a granite sarcophagus. On it lay a mummified foot, looking rather like an old, grubby football sock.

Out of the gloom came a hissing sound. A big, square-shouldered man came walking sideways on to the screen and stopped in front of the mummified foot. He wore a white kilt over his tree-trunk legs and had a deeply tanned bare chest. An impossibly tiny serpent's head and neck sprang from his shoulders, and, in profile, a single serpent's eye stared at the players unblinkingly. As he hissed, a forked tongue made pink lightning in front of his snake-mouth. Words appeared in a box on the screen.

THIS IS THE SNAKE-HEADED ONE. TO GAIN THE FOOT OF OSIRIS, YOU MUST ANSWER HIS QUESTION. DO YOU SEE THIS SARCOPHAGUS? YOU MUST GUESS THE IDENTITY OF THE MUMMY INSIDE IT. HERE IS YOUR CLUE. THE MUMMY BELONGS TO HIM ... BUT IN WHAT WAY? LISTEN TO WHAT HE SAYS, BUT HURRY. YOU HAVE ONLY MOMENTS TO SOLVE THE PUZZLE.

I AM THE CHILD OF MY MUMMY,
YET THIS IS NOT MY MUMMY INSIDE.
THIS MUMMY NO LONGER LIVES,
YET MY MUMMY HASN'T DIED.
WHO THEN IS MY MUMMY? ... QUICK,
YOU MUST DECIDE!

I AM THE CHILD OF MY MUMMY,
BUT MY MUMMY NEVER GAVE BIRTH.
MY MUMMY IS NOW DEAD,
YET MY MUMMY STILL WALKS THE EARTH.
WHO THEN IS MY MUMMY? ... QUICK,
YOU MUST USE YOUR HEAD!

"How are we supposed to know?" Josh complained. "Pity we've already got a box up on the screen. We need another one. Funny, these boxes don't help you when you really need help."

"Don't be rude about the game," Harry said.

"You think the game's on our side, do you?" Josh was irritated by Harry's trust in it. "Games and machines aren't on anybody's side and neither is this one. All it wants to do is beat us. Games haven't got feelings."

"I'm not so sure," Amy said. "I think this game does have feelings. And they're not always very nice feelings. I think this game's a bit evil ..."

"But it can't be!" Harry protested. "It's *fun*!"

Fun. That explained Harry, Josh thought. Harry was afraid of nothing, because everything was fun to him. He looked at their snake-headed challenger. He wanted to beat him. But how? The riddle had him baffled.

"That clue's a load of dummy mummy nonsense," he

said finally. "Maybe it deserves a nonsense answer." He decided to ignore the fact that it was really Amy's turn. "I've got it! The one inside that coffin isn't a mummy at all—it's his daddy."

"No, that couldn't be the answer," Amy said. "That *is* nonsense. Egyptians wouldn't twist words like 'mummy' and 'daddy'."

"That's where you're wrong," Harry said. "Ancient Egyptians loved playing tricks with words."

As he said this, another box appeared on the screen.

EGYPTIAN LANGUAGE USAGE WAS RICH IN PUNS AND WORD PLAY. MANY EGYPTIAN WORDS HAD TWO MEANINGS. THE WORD "PHARAOH", FOR EXAMPLE, MEANT "GREAT HOUSE" OR "THE KING" ... WORDS WERE THINGS TO THE EGYPTIANS, AND IF TWO WORDS HAD SIMILAR SOUNDS, THEN THEY MUST HAVE SOME CONNECTION.

"Another of those boring boxes when we don't want them," Josh said.

"No, I think you've got it," Harry said. "The mummy is his father."

"Shall I type in the answer?" Amy said to Harry.

"Yes."

Amy's fingers rattled away at the keyboard.

New words appeared in the box.

CORRECT. THE MUMMY IN THE SARCOPHAGUS IS THE SNAKE-HEADED ONE'S FATHER. WELL SOLVED. YOU HAVE GAINED THE FOOT OF OSIRIS.

The snake-headed one gave an angry hiss. In a flash

he turned into a snake and wriggled away into the darkness. At the same time, a shimmering light grew around the foot, which then faded and disappeared.

"You did it, Josh! You were right!" Harry cheered. "We've solved the first challenge."

"I don't believe it," Josh said, looking stunned.

"Neither do I," Amy said. "That was an absolute fluke."

"No it wasn't." Josh tried to bluff. "You know me. I've played a lot of computer games. I know how they work."

Amy's big, clear grey eyes looked right into him. "Be honest."

"I solved it, didn't I?"

"By accident."

"Who says?"

"You always have to win, don't you?"

"I don't always win. You solved the puzzle of the doorway."

"And you hated it."

Harry lost his look of admiration. "Is she right, Josh? Was it just a lucky guess?"

"Don't *you* start," Josh said.

"I think we've played enough," Amy said. "I want to write my project."

"But we can't stop now," Harry said. "We're going great."

"I'm not playing with people who won't be honest."

Harry turned a pleading look on Josh.

Josh felt cornered. "What does she want me to say? It was a guess? Okay, it was a guess. Every answer's a guess. After all, you don't know if you're right, do you?"

"It wasn't even a guess," Amy said. "It was a lucky accident."

Josh knew the warning look on his sister's face. She'd stop them playing this game if he didn't back down, and she could force it, too. One word to their mother about Josh playing computer games and that would be the end of the game, and maybe the end of all computer games for a while.

"Call it lucky if you like. It certainly was lucky, seeing I got the answer right. Anyway, who cares?"

Amy said: "I do."

Josh felt his anger build. Did she have to make such a fuss about it?

"Can we play on later—one more stage?" Harry pleaded.

"Maybe tomorrow, but not for long. I want the computer tomorrow night."

A box came up on the screen.

> DON'T DELAY TOO LONG. YOUR NEXT CHALLENGE IS TO FIND THE SECOND FOOT OF OSIRIS. A WARNING: ONCE YOU HAVE STARTED PLAYING THIS GAME, YOU WON'T BE ABLE TO STOP. YOU MAY HAVE A BREAK AFTER EACH CHALLENGE, BUT THE LONGER YOU DELAY, THE MORE MUMMY MONSTERS WILL BE SET LOOSE TO CHALLENGE YOU ... AND THEY WILL BECOME SCARIER AND SCARIER ...

"Turn it off now," Amy demanded, taking charge.

"But—" Josh began.

"Harry said the game had a memory, so turn it off."

Josh glared at her. Harry obeyed, quitting the programme. The machine gave a *ping* and spat out the disk.
Harry switched off the computer.

Amy jumped up and opened the curtains. Afternoon
light streamed into Josh's bedroom and made them
all blink.

Amy picked up the ginger cat from the end of
the bed.

"Come on, Spy, let's go out of this stuffy room and get
some fresh air." She gave the cat a cuddle, and he purred
in her arms with the sound of a small, muffled motor.

Josh pushed himself angrily away from the desk.
What a dumb decision to stop now, he thought. He
wanted to have his turn at the controls. Now he would
have to wait, and he didn't like waiting.

Amy was being a pain.

Josh went for a ride around the block on his skateboard.
He liked to skate. It calmed him when he was feeling
angry, and it helped him to think, especially about
games. He bent low over the board to capture speed,
powering along with one foot.

The skateboard was a wide blue one, a bit old-
fashioned. Josh preferred the wide boards and didn't
approve of the newer narrow models. His board had
high-profile urethane wheels, not the new wheels with
urethane so thin that it barely covered the bearings. He
enjoyed the feeling of sailing high above the pavement.
Balancing on the board helped him to slice through
problems, to lead his thoughts in a clear line.

The Mummy Monster Game was very mysterious.

Did Harry have other games like this? Josh wondered about that shop in Cairo.

He worked his way up a rise, thrusting with one foot, shifting his weight, yet keeping a smooth course. He went over the rise and picked up speed on the other side. The breeze whipped cleanly past his face.

The game was going to test him. He felt a twinge of anxiety. *What if I'm not as good as I think I am, and I show myself up? What will Harry think if I lose my nerve and I slip up?* Harry didn't seem to have any nerves. He was smug and safe, as if he were protected by some kind of invisible armour. Fear couldn't get to Harry. Was it because he was younger? No, it must be more than that. Josh could not remember ever feeling as safe and comfortable as Harry. He'd learnt as a small child, when his father had left home, that the world was not always something he could control. Maybe life had been too good to Harry. He wondered what it would take to change him.

He saw a boy on a skateboard up ahead, pumping himself along with a sneakered foot. New kid on the block. Josh had seen him once or twice but had never bothered to speak to him. *I'll show him.* Josh moved out and flashed past the boy, leaving him turning his head in surprise.

Josh didn't look back. He sailed past some houses and along the edge of the local park. Should he go into the park? No, a council inspector might catch him. They didn't like skateboarders in the park. It was a pity. The park was divided by smooth concrete paths and a single road with some interesting speed humps along its length. Josh usually skated there in the evenings when it was quiet. Sometimes he took his mother's dog Tina for a run behind him.

He turned the corner and headed back towards home.

They were watching television in the family room downstairs. Amy and Harry sat on the couch. Amy was stroking Spy on her lap. Josh lounged in a chair with his leg slung over the arm.

Tina gave a whine and jumped on to the couch. She was a miniature white poodle, clipped like a fancy hedge. She looked enviously at the cat in Amy's arms, and licked Amy's elbow.

"Not now, Tina. I'm busy giving Spy a love."

Their mother was late home from work. There was nothing unusual in this. Josh and Amy were used to eating late. But Harry was getting hungry.

"When do we eat?"

Josh wondered if he should start getting dinner ready. Josh, Amy and their mother took turns preparing the evening meal, except on those nights when Mum decided to pick up takeaway on the way home. Josh quite enjoyed cooking. It had its advantages, too: you could taste the food as often as you liked without anyone grumbling at you, and it also meant that someone else had to stack the dishwasher. Josh was a better cook than Amy, or so he felt. He was famous for his spaghetti bolognaise.

"Where's your mother?" Harry asked.

"Working."

"This late? Doesn't she ever come home?"

"She works very hard for us," Amy said defensively.

"At least she's here and not in Egypt like your mother," Josh said.

The phone rang, and Amy answered it.

"Mum. No we haven't. Oh good—you're bringing pizza home." She smiled over her shoulder at the boys. "Great! Ham and pineapple, please. No, we're just watching TV. Homework? Of course I'll do it. I always do. Oh, you mean Josh. I don't know about him. But I've brought home my science project to show you. You can't? But you're always bringing work home! All right, maybe tomorrow night … I got top marks …" She was quiet for a moment, then turned again to the boys. "Mum has to bring work home tonight. She wants to know if she should pick up a video for us. What would you like? Harry, you're our guest, so you're allowed to choose."

Harry chose a horror movie called *Blood from the Mummy's Tomb*.

Amy passed his request on to her mother and said goodbye.

"I think I'll do some homework," she said, putting down the receiver. "I don't want to watch the movie."

"I'm not watching it alone," Harry said firmly.

Josh looked at him in surprise. Was Harry actually scared of something? This was too good a chance to miss. He growled deep in his throat. "You don't have to be scared of horror movies, Harry," he said.

Harry looked concerned.

"That's mean, Josh," Amy said.

"All right," Josh said, softening. "Sorry, Harry. Only

kidding. We'll watch it with you."

"Good. I wouldn't want you to miss it," Harry said in a matter-of-fact voice. "You see, *Blood from the Mummy's Tomb* will help you enjoy the Mummy Monster Game even more. It's great fun. I've seen it six times. I love watching it alone at night in my mother's study with all her Egyptian statues and painted masks on the walls looking down at me!"

Harry wasn't scared at all. Josh should have known. Pity, though, he thought. Harry had seemed human for a moment, and he'd almost warmed to him.

The sound of a car horn tooting outside announced the arrival of their mother. The car crunched up the gravel driveway. Tina ran to the front door, barking. Their mother came into the family room carrying a big pizza box and a video.

"Hello, family. Hello, Harry. How have you enjoyed your first day here? Sorry I had to work late."

She brought a breeze of perfume—and pizza—into the room. Amy hugged her and Josh took the pizza box and the video from her hands. She kicked off her shoes and pulled off her earrings, spilling them on to a cabinet.

"Hello, Aunt Helen." Harry's smile widened at the sight of the pizza box. Josh put it and the video on a small coffee table and they all gathered around.

Amy opened the box. The pizza looked and smelled great, Josh thought, but the cover of the video was enough to put him off his food. It showed a mummy's tomb with a trickle of blood emerging from it. Amy must have been thinking the same thing, because she tucked the video under the table, out of sight. Harry was too busy looking at the pizza to notice. His eyes shone.

"So what have you three been doing this afternoon?" their mother said to Harry.

"It's been great, Aunt Helen, we've been playing a computer game."

Josh gave him a warning glare.

His mother rounded on Josh. "Don't tell me you've been wasting time playing your computer games again! You've got homework to do, and I'm tired of hearing complaints from your school."

"No, it was *my* game—" Harry began to explain.

"Then he *has* been playing computer games!" Josh's cool, businesslike mum suddenly snapped. "Josh, I've told you a thousand times about wasting time on computer games! I didn't buy you and Amy the computer so you'd neglect your homework. You disappoint me sometimes! I think I make a big mistake being so soft with you and buying you all the things you want. Honestly, you promised me!"

Their mother was usually calm, but she had a secret anger locked away inside her, like the old album that she kept locked in a trunk. It contained her wedding photographs and photographs of the husband who had left her when the children were much smaller. When her anger came out, it did so in a torrent. Usually she was angry about the children and how they were managing their lives. Amy said it was because she had to be very cool and competent all day. When she allowed herself to be upset, the pressure pushed the words out of her in a flood.

Harry gave Josh an awkward, apologetic smile. *Sorry*, the look said. *I didn't mean to drop you into such a heap of trouble.*

Amy's face had darkened. "*I* don't waste my time playing games on the computer," she said in a small, angry voice. "I've done three of my school projects on the computer this year, but you haven't even looked at them. You'd rather shout at Josh for not doing his homework! Maybe you'd pay more attention to me if I *did* play computer games all the time!"

Harry gulped. Now he'd started a family row.

Amy always felt that her achievements were over-looked. She shut herself in her bedroom for hours, working herself white in the face over schoolwork, but her mother never seemed to give her the approval she wanted. It didn't stop Amy, though. She just tried even harder. But anger had a way of suddenly bursting out of her, too.

Their mother calmed down. "I'm sorry, Amy. I know you work hard. Unfortunately I've also had to work very hard lately. And it isn't getting any easier." She smiled at Harry to lighten the situation, regretting her outburst in front of him. "Sorry, Harry. We don't squabble like this all the time. We're all tired and hungry. Let's eat."

For a few minutes all conversation became stuck in strings of melted mozzarella cheese. The hungry children's priority was to keep up with each other. They went clockwise around the pizza, working their way through the segments faster than a sweep second hand on a stopwatch, and their mother wisely moved in from an anti-clockwise direction. Josh calculated that they ought to meet and touch fingers with her at about twenty to twelve. He had to race to keep up with Harry. For a smaller kid, he could bolt down pizza, that was for sure. Tina, the poodle, looked on with interest.

At last their mother sighed with satisfaction. "That'll do me. Did you walk Tina for me today, Josh?"

It was Josh's job, along with taking out the garbage, to walk Tina. He liked to go on his skateboard, trailing the dog behind him on an extended lead.

"Not today, Mum."

"Do it tomorrow, will you?"

"I'll remind you," Harry said through a mouthful of ham and pineapple, trying to make up for having landed Josh in trouble.

After their meal, the children settled down to watch *Blood from the Mummy's Tomb*. It was a spooky movie about an ancient Egyptian princess who was reborn as a modern girl.

During a quiet, tense moment in the film, when the characters were examining a tomb, Josh heard a scraping sound on the windowsill behind the video recorder. Harry stiffened. Spy stirred in Amy's lap and twitched his ears. Something, hidden by the edge of the curtain, was crawling along the sill. Josh and Amy looked at each other. *Scrape, scrape, scrape.* What could it be? Was it inside the room, behind the curtain? Or outside in the dark?

In his mind Josh pictured a giant with the head of a crocodile and jaws wrapped in tattered bandages. *Scrape,*

scrape. He tensed.

Something came scraping and scurrying along the wooden sill. It was a beetle about the size of a walnut.

Josh snorted inwardly at his fears. Was that all?

"That's strange," Harry said. He jumped up for a closer look. "Wow! It looks just like an Egyptian scarab beetle!"

The beetle was dark, the colour of anthracite, and shone with a greenish tinge in the light of a standard lamp near the window. As Harry bent to examine it, the beetle opened its wing cases. Harry jumped. The beetle buzzed out of the room, grinding the air with its wings.

"I wonder if it was a scarab beetle," Harry said, climbing back on to the couch.

"It's just a normal beetle," Josh told him. "We've got heaps of them in the garden. They come inside because they're attracted by the light."

Harry wasn't convinced. "Maybe. But it looked just like a scarab to me."

Amy exchanged a questioning glance with Josh. Maybe horror movies really did scare Harry, after all. "If this movie's too spooky for you, Harry, just say so and we'll switch it off," she said. "Does your mother know you watch movies like this?"

"Of course she does. She doesn't think this is a scary movie. She thinks it's funny."

Josh supposed that Aunt Jillian was just as fearless as Harry. Josh and Amy didn't see much of her because she was always in Egypt on some archaeological project. He remembered her as a tall woman with a big, flashing smile. Above all, he remembered her voice, a whispery voice that seemed to be sharing a secret with them, no matter what she was telling them. Harry had shown them a recent snapshot of his mother taken at an Egyptian site. Aunt Jillian was dressed in khaki field clothes and was leaning against a temple column, squinting in the sunlight. Josh admired her adventurous air, and he felt a stab of envy for Harry that made him feel disloyal to his own mother. He felt drawn to Aunt Jillian. She did exciting things—like Josh's father, who used to take him on camping expeditions in his four-wheel-drive when he was a small boy. Josh missed real adventure in his life. He hoped that one day he'd get to spend more time with his mysterious Aunt Jillian.

They sat back again to watch the movie, all except Harry. Harry couldn't settle. He fidgeted, picked at the arm of the couch, kicked his legs. Josh stole a glance at him. Harry didn't look at all scared. He looked excited. He was probably thinking of the game waiting for them upstairs.

6

Leaks

"Time for school," Josh's mother called, putting her head in at the door of his bedroom. "You've taken so long to get up that Amy's beaten you into the shower."

"Then I can sleep for another hour," he said into his pillow. "She'll be that long."

"Up!" his mother said.

Tina bounced into the room, stood on her back legs and licked Josh's face.

"Stop it, Tina, it's not my turn to shower yet." He was about to push the dog's paws off the bed when she gave a small growl and scooted across the carpet to his wardrobe. She scratched at the sliding door.

"Out of my wardrobe!" Josh called.

"She's probably trying to tell you to tidy it," his mother said. "Come on, Tina." But the dog wouldn't listen. She whined at the wardrobe door. "Out, Tina! You don't want to look in there. The shock of Josh's wardrobe would be too much for a delicate creature like you." She bent and swept the dog up in her arms. "Get up now, Josh."

Josh lay in bed, thinking of the Mummy Monster

Game. No game had ever loomed quite so large in his mind as this one. He had dreamed about it all night. He blinked sleepily at the computer monitor on his desk. The game had brought something exciting into his life. He had felt as if he'd been part of it, as if he'd been swept up in the action. They had all felt it. Why? The graphics and sound quality were excellent, that was true. But there was more to it than that.

Sun streamed into his bedroom and fell in yellow patches on the carpet. Motes of dust, kicked up by the poodle's scampering paws, floated in the sunlight, making vague shapes in the air like dust phantoms.

The game was alive, somehow. It possessed an hypnotic quality that made them believe that they were caught up in the action.

Virtual reality. That was it. Maybe this was one of the new generation of amazing virtual reality games.

Wow, Josh thought. What luck that I've got the chance to play it.

The Mummy Monster Game had the power to throw shadows. It could change the temperature of the air. It could give those who played it the sensation of passing through stone-walled passages that pressed coldly around them, and it could make the floor seem to tremble. Most scary of all, it exerted a pull on their senses as if it were actually drawing them *into* it, really making them experience its challenges.

Josh remembered the wailing figure of Isis, the horrible mummy monster with the crocodile jaws, the barechested snake-headed one hissing, his tongue flickering.

He wondered what challenge they would have to

overcome to gain the next fragment, the second foot of Osiris.

He could hardly wait to play again.

Josh took a long shower.

Afterwards, he padded back into his room, a big white towel wrapped around his stocky body, his black hair clinging wetly to his face. He was surprised to find his mother in his bedroom.

"I thought I'd come and take a look at this mess while you were safely out of the way," she said. She had opened his wardrobe and was staring at something sticking out from beneath a raincoat.

Josh gulped. It looked like a bandaged mummified foot.

Would she scream?

She did.

"Look at this old football sock, Josh! It's disgusting! I'm not picking up your mess, do you hear me?" she shouted. Then she stamped out of his room and closed the door after her.

Josh crouched to peer at the mysterious object.

Harry must be playing a trick. He'd hidden a mummy's foot in Josh's wardrobe, hoping to scare him to death. But where had it come from? Perhaps he'd brought it back from Egypt after one of his visits. Or maybe Aunt Jillian had sent it to him. Pest! He was probably lying in bed next door in the guest bedroom, trying not to laugh, waiting to hear Josh's yell of terror.

The foot was withered and a yellowish-brown in colour like cornflakes. It was also blackened in places as if streaked with Vegemite.

Maybe there was more than just a foot peeking out from behind the raincoat. Josh shrank back. Maybe there was a whole mummy concealed in his wardrobe.

The words of warning that came with the game returned to prod him like an icy finger. *Be warned: the longer you take to complete the quest, the more mummy monsters will be set loose to challenge you!*

The droplets of shower water on his body turned icy cold.

Calm down, he told himself. *The Mummy Monster Game is just a game. This reaction is exactly what Harry will be hoping for.*

He wouldn't be scared by something that looked like an old footy sock.

He leaned into the wardrobe, twitched the raincoat aside. Behind it was a blank white wall. No mummy. Josh gave a shivery sigh of relief, and looked down at the foot.

What? It had changed! It wasn't a mummy's foot any more. It *was* just a dirty old footy sock.

I know what I saw, he thought. *It wasn't this.*

Josh wondered about it as he dressed. He had heard of people having hallucinations. Could something look as real as that in an hallucination? What had caused it? It had to be something to do with the game. He decided to talk to Harry.

He opened the door of Harry's bedroom. His cousin was sound asleep, hugging his pillow as if it were a teddy bear.

"Harry, I want to talk to you."

Harry sat up, rubbing his eyes. "Hi, Josh. What's the matter?"

"It's that game of yours."

"What about it?"

"It's messing me up. I saw something in my wardrobe."

"What?"

"Don't laugh. A bandaged foot. It just appeared."

"A mummy's foot?" Harry was wide awake now. His bright blue eyes shone like high-wattage globes. "Is it still there?"

"No, there's only a footy sock there now. But I saw what I saw."

"Then that's the second thing. Remember the beetle last night?" Josh had forgotten about the beetle. "The game says it lets things loose to challenge us. Maybe it lets things loose into our lives. It's haunting us." He sat up excitedly. "Great!"

"I don't think it's great at all. I don't like mummies in my bedroom, not even my own, my mother—who, by the way, was in my bedroom a moment ago and could easily have seen the foot—but especially not the mummy of some creepy dead Egyptian king. Maybe we should stop playing this game."

"We can't do that," Harry said quickly.

"Why not?"

"The game says we can't. If we stop playing, more things will be let loose. You could find something worse in your wardrobe tomorrow, like that big guy with the crocodile head."

"This is crazy. Or else the game's sending us crazy."

"No it isn't. These Egyptian games are a bit

surprising, that's all. We just have to finish it. Don't let it spook you, Josh," Harry said soothingly. "It only makes things more exciting."

"You think so?"

"Yeah. You're not scared, are you?"

The look on Harry's face challenged him, dared him to admit his fear. Josh glared at him. He had to show this kid. He'd keep on playing for as long as Harry did—and then a bit more. No computer game was going to beat him.

"Who's scared?"

"Good. As soon as we've put Osiris together again, it'll all stop. But don't tell anyone about the foot, especially not Amy."

"Amy would freak out," Josh said.

"Best if she doesn't know," Harry said wisely. "When you come back from school, we can play some more."

Josh and Amy sat at the kitchen table eating their corn-flakes. Their mother came into the kitchen to pour herself a cup of coffee. She never ate breakfast.

"Hello, kids."

"Morning, Mummy," Amy said appeasingly, trying to make up for her outburst of the night before.

At the word "mummy", Josh's spoon fell out of his hand and hit the edge of his bowl with a sharp *clink*.

"What's the matter, Josh?" Amy said, frowning at him.

"He's probably jumpy because he hasn't done his homework and he's scared of going to school," their mother said, filling a cup with coffee from the coffee-maker. "Well, I'm not writing any excuse notes for you,

Josh. I've told you not to spend so much time playing computer games. If I hear one more complaint from your teacher, I'm confiscating your computer for a whole week."

"You can't—"

"Watch me."

"I mean ..."

"You can't confiscate it," Amy said. "I've got to write my play."

"Play?"

"I told you, Mummy. I'm writing a play for drama. It's going to be performed by our class. I hope you're going to come and see it."

"Just remember what I said, Josh," his mother said, going out with the cup of coffee in her hand.

"What?—oh yeah." He lowered his voice to a tense whisper. "Why do you call her Mummy all the time? Don't you think you're too big to be saying Mummy?"

"It hasn't bothered you before. What's wrong with 'Mummy' all of a sudden?" Comprehension dawned in Amy's shrewd grey eyes. "Harry's computer game is getting to you. Is that it? Has my big brother got a bit sensitive about mummies?"

Josh watched Amy finish her cornflakes and then go on to a slice of toast and Vegemite. He pushed his own bowl away. He didn't feel hungry.

He wished he could tell Amy what he'd seen, but she was eating happily. No, it would definitely freak her out.

The morning at school went by in a blur for Josh. They had a history lesson on ancient Egypt, but he hardly heard a word, although he did remember his teacher saying that the class would be going on an excursion to the city museum within the next few days.

All he could think about was the horrific object he had seen in his bedroom. Would more things appear? He should never have started playing this game. His mother had been right: playing computer games all the time was bad for you. You started to lose all sense of reality.

The Mummy Monster Game was astonishing, though. Its excitement created in him a hunger, a yearning for more. For all his feeling of dread, he longed to be back playing it.

He looked around the class at the other pupils. They looked normal. Well, all except Freaky Freddie Maloney. What would they say if they knew what had appeared in his wardrobe?

They wouldn't believe it.

Did he?

7

Seeing Things

Amy ran across the sportsfield to where Josh sat on the grass with a group of friends. They were all computer gameheads and Josh was their champion.

They were talking about their latest games. Josh was dying to tell them about the Mummy Monster Game, but he thought better of it.

Amy was pale and wild-looking.

"What's up, Sis?"

She took him aside. "Come and have a look right now. I don't know what's in my satchel, but it's not very funny. Did you put it there?" she said all in a rush, the way their mother did when she was upset.

"What do you mean?"

"Come."

She led him to the school lockers. "That's mine," she said, pointing.

"I know that," Josh said. "So open it."

"No thanks. *You* open it. Look inside my satchel."

Josh looked at the closed metal door. He felt the presence of something behind it, something lying coiled and waiting like a snake. A picture of his bedroom wardrobe dropped into his mind like a slide into a projector. He saw again the secret horror that had been inside it, half hidden by the raincoat. Why was he thinking of that? This was a school locker—his sister's. There was nothing to be scared of. They weren't playing the game now. Cautiously he opened the door.

Amy's satchel was at the bottom of the locker, lying on its side.

"Open it," Amy said.

Josh picked up the satchel, pulled back the flap, and peered inside.

He looked at Amy in puzzlement.

He turned the satchel upside down.

Out dropped a dingy white sneaker, discoloured from use on the school's clay tennis courts.

"That's not what I saw," Amy said, blinking at it. "I know what I saw. It was a horrible thing—a disgusting old withered foot wrapped in yukky bandages!"

"A mummy's foot," Josh suggested.

"Yes, that's what it looked like. How did you know?"

"I thought I saw one today, too." He told her then about the football sock, and about his fears. "I didn't say anything in case I'd imagined it. The game warned us that it lets things loose."

Amy didn't freak out as Josh had expected. She didn't even question his explanation. She knew what she had seen in her satchel, and she was coldly angry.

"Thanks a lot, Josh!" she said. "You knew something creepy was happening and you kept it from me. Why weren't you honest with me?"

"I didn't want to scare you."

"You're scaring me now. What else has happened? Tell me this very second or I'll never trust you again."

"Nothing."

Amy came to a decision. "We've got to stop playing the game."

"We can't, Amy." He explained what might happen if they stopped now, how even worse things might start appearing.

"Worse things than a mummy's foot in my school satchel?" His sister's clear eyes darkened at the prospect. "I don't like this, Josh. You mean this game has got hold of our lives? We've got to keep playing till we've finished it?"

"That's what Harry says."

"Well, I'm not going to play it any more. The game is bad. It's affecting us, and I'm scared."

"Harry's not scared. Are we going to let him be braver than we are? He's testing us. Let's show him. I'd like to beat Harry at his own game."

"That's your trouble, Josh. You always want to show everybody how good you are. But computer games don't matter."

"They do to me."

"I wish I knew why."

"Because I'm good at them, and that makes me feel good," he said. "Anyway, who are you to talk? You want to show everybody how clever you are, too. That's why you knock yourself out doing homework."

"That's different. Hard work at school is going to get me somewhere one day, not like stupid computer games that mess up your brain."

"Computer games are fun!"

"You're starting to sound like Harry."

Amy made Josh carry her satchel home from school, and she walked a few paces ahead of him.

"What a kind brother," a girl from Josh's class said teasingly, noticing that Amy was walking empty-handed. "Carrying little sister's bag home for her, are we?"

Josh glared at her. He wished there really was a mummified foot inside the satchel. He'd like to have taken it out and waggled it under the girl's nose. But he shrugged the irritation aside.

All he wanted to do now was hurry back to the game. He had a history essay to write this afternoon, but he pushed it out of his mind. The game came first.

When they reached home Tina met them at the door, yapping excitedly.

"Hello, Tina-weena," Amy said. "Where's Spy?" The ginger cat was usually to be found in the hallway at this time of day, watching the door for Amy's arrival.

"Spy! Here, kitty-kit-kit!"

There was no sign of Spy—or of Harry, Josh noted. He'd better not be playing the computer game without us, he thought. He ran upstairs to look for Harry while Amy went through the kitchen and out into the back garden to look for Spy.

Josh found his bedroom door closed. When he opened it, he found that the room was in darkness. Peering through the gloom, he saw Harry crouching on the floor, his head hidden under the bed.

"Harry! What are you doing in my room? And what are you doing under the bed?"

Harry's head emerged. "I'm looking for Spy. He's vanished." He climbed to his feet. "I was playing the game, Josh, and Spy came in to spy on me, but something's gone badly wrong …"

"What do you mean? You've been playing the game without us?" Josh said angrily.

"Yes, yes, but it's changed. It isn't the way it was before. Those lines appeared on the screen again. Maybe they made me dizzy, I don't know, but I'll swear they drew me in. The game became real. You should have seen it! I was pulled into a maze, and Spy was pulled in with me. There were walls of stone all around us. Lots of them. We were trapped. I couldn't tell where I was going." Harry's eyes were shining with excitement.

Josh pushed past him and drew back the curtains.

Nothing in the bedroom seemed to have changed.

"Have you flipped out, Harry?"

"No, of course I haven't. Don't you believe me? It frightened the cat silly, being pulled in like that. Poor Spy—his fur stood up on his back and he spat like mad."

"So where is Spy now?"

"I don't know. I've looked everywhere. He was running with me through the maze. Then I saw him take off along one of the passages. He saw a mummified mouse. I tried to follow him, but I lost sight of him."

"Maybe he ran out the bedroom door."

"The door was closed. I closed it after he came in. What have I done, Josh? Spy's lost!" Harry's eyes grew round. "Oh, boy, what's Amy going to say!"

"He can't be lost," Josh said. "The game's got you spooked, Harry. You should never have played on without us." Vainly Josh searched the bedroom, even crawling under the bed. "Here, Spy ... ksk, ksk, ksk!"

"He's gone," Harry said in a small voice.

Amy came up the stairs, looking distant. "'Lo, Harry."

"Hi, Amy. I've been playing the game while you were at school," Harry told her. "I won back the other mummy foot of Osiris, and after that—"

"Don't talk to me about it," Amy said. She flashed a look of dread at the computer on Josh's desk.

"What's the matter?" Harry said.

"Tell him," Amy said to Josh.

"Another mummy foot appeared—in Amy's satchel."

"Ah, I see. Sorry, Amy. But that's not all. I've just been through a maze, and I won the first leg of Osiris. It popped up too. It appeared in the room, hanging down from the bedcovers, or so I thought at first, but it turned out to be a sheet. We're about to go for the other leg."

Amy went into her bedroom and slammed the door.

Harry looked surprised. "Doesn't she want to play?"

"No. And you've jumped your turn," Josh said grumpily. "I was supposed to be next."

"Sorry, I couldn't wait. You see, other things were coming through. I've seen more scarab beetles, and there was a huge scorpion in the passageway. I nearly stepped on it, and Spy chased it outside. Do you remember what the game said? The longer we take, the more mummy monsters will be set loose against us. We can't waste time."

"What did you have to do to win the other foot?" Josh asked.

"I had to pick my way through a hall full of stone sphinxes lying on slabs. Except they weren't all made of stone, as I discovered. Some were real lions. That's when the game started to change. It really felt as if I was right there in the hall, because when I crept past one of the sphinxes, something happened. I saw the tip of its tail give a twitch. Then it roared, jumped up from its slab, and swung at me with its claws. I soon learnt to watch their tails! I only just got out of the way in time. Look!" He pointed to a neat slit in the sleeve of his shirt.

"You could have ripped that on something else."

"I didn't!" Harry said, exasperated. "Wait till you play again, Josh. You'll see!"

"We'll have to play on and try to get Spy back," Josh said. "We'll play without Amy."

"I wouldn't advise it," Harry said. "We need to use all of our brain power. I nearly messed up this morning in the hall of sphinxes, and then in the maze. I wished you'd both been here."

Perhaps he was right. Josh remembered how Amy had solved the problem about the house of eternity. Without her help, the game would have ended right there.

But how would she take the news about Spy?

He went to Amy's bedroom. She had locked her door. Josh tapped on it.

"Come and play with us, Amy."

The voice inside sounded very small and lonely. "Go away, Josh. It's a horrible game. I don't want to hear about it any more."

"We need you."

"I told you, I don't want to play."

"Please."

"You're the computer game expert," Josh heard her say. "You don't need me."

"But we do need you." Josh disliked giving Amy credit for showing skill at computer games—computer games were his passion—but suddenly he shared a certainty with Harry that they needed Amy if they were going to complete the quest. He didn't want to go back into his bedroom and play the game only with Harry. Amy's presence was reassuring, steadying. And Harry was right: they were going to need their combined brain power to defeat the scary reality of the Mummy Monster Game. "You're good, and we're going to need all three of us to play."

"No."

"Then there's something I have to tell you. Spy has gone. Harry says a maze inside the game just swallowed him up. He saw Spy running off into a passage. Now he's vanished."

That brought Amy out fast. "What are you telling me, Josh?"

"Spy's lost, we think."

His sister's wail of anguish reminded Josh of Isis in the burial chamber. Amy rushed into Josh's bedroom. "Harry, what have you done with my cat? Tell me!"

Harry told her his amazing story.

"This isn't a trick to make me play, is it?" she said.

"I wish it was a trick," Harry said guiltily. "Sorry, Amy."

"I knew this game was evil!" Amy said with a shake of anger in her voice.

"Perhaps Harry doesn't think the game's so safe now," Josh said to Amy, remembering how Harry had trusted it.

"You had to play this game, didn't you!" Amy snapped back at him. "Now this has happened! My poor little Spy! We've got to do something. We've got to tell Mum."

"What's the point?" Josh said. "She'll just stop us from playing. Then we'll never get Spy back."

"And it won't stop things haunting us," Harry said. "I think this game means what it says. It's got hold of us now, and it's going to keep making things tougher."

"It's trying to scare us," Josh said.

"Well, it's not having Spy!" Amy said fiercely.

Josh pictured the frightened animal flitting through the Egyptian passages like a ginger shadow. Would they ever get him back?

Harry drew the curtains again and the three settled down in front of the computer for the next challenge.

"It's my turn," Josh reminded them.

Harry handed him the controls without argument.

The glowing lines of a passage, converging in infinity, appeared in front of them, drawing their eyes to the centre of the screen. At first they were aware of the three adventurers hiking along the stone-walled corridor, but soon it seemed that they moved through and beyond them. The coldness of the stone seeped through their clothing. Josh shivered.

"I wonder what surprise this thing's got for us next,"

Amy said. She glared at the pulsating lines, trying to resist their hypnotic pull.

"Yes, I wonder," Josh agreed. "How about showing us one of those stupid boxes?" he said to the screen in a rather demanding way.

A panel with words came up.

> CERTAIN PEOPLE COMPLAIN ABOUT THESE BOXES COMING UP WHEN THEY DON'T NEED THEM. IF THEY DON'T WANT THEIR HELP, THEY SHOULDN'T ASK QUESTIONS. IF THEY DO, THEY SHOULD SAY "SORRY".

Josh blinked in surprise. "Sorry," he said.

"The game's touchy," Harry whispered.

The square on the screen went blank, seemed to be thinking. The disk drive beside the computer gave a grunt, then hummed in a thoughtful way. Then more words appeared over the screen.

> THE NEXT FRAGMENT YOU MUST DISCOVER IS THE SECOND LEG OF OSIRIS. IT IS GUARDED BY A TERRIBLE VULTURE-HEADED GODDESS NAMED NEKHBET. SHE WILL ATTACK YOU IF YOU CANNOT OVERCOME HER CHALLENGE.

Josh's hands on the controls went damp. He moved the joystick and pressed on along the stone passageway.

Perhaps the game had warmed up after Harry's adventures in the hall of sphinxes and the maze. The glowing lines of the passage brightened and began to hum and then whine, as if the game had reached a new pitch of intensity.

Then, with startling suddenness, like a spacecraft going into hyper-space in a science-fiction movie, the lines accelerated and blasted to the centre of the screen. Josh was yanked out of his chair as if pulled by strings.

The screen vanished. The controls vanished. Josh flew.

He rushed through a cold length of stone, the lines streaming past him like neon strips. He looked to one side. The others were flying too. Amy's mouth was open and there was a look of horror on her face. Harry's lips were drawn back in a grin.

They came to a pinpoint of light that flashed. Their feet hit the floor. They had landed in a stone passage!

Amy screamed, a twisted, echoing sound in the narrow corridor.

"Oh wow!" Harry yelled.

Josh felt his feet pounding on the stone. He was running, and he didn't seem to have the power to stop. Momentum, or some magnetic force, carried him on. The others were running beside him.

Then the passage ended, and they found that they had run into a bird cage—a giant bird cage with bars as thick as telephone poles.

They stopped. Harry pointed upwards, and Amy and Josh tilted their heads to follow his line of vision. A woman with a white vulture's head and wings sat above them on a perch that was the thickness of a tree trunk. Below her the second leg of Osiris lay on an altar.

With a great whistling of wings, the bird-woman flew to the floor of the cage. She spoke in a cawing voice:

"I AM NEKHBET, THE VULTURE GODDESS OF NEKHEN.

TO RECOVER THE SECOND LEG OF OSIRIS, YOU MUST SOLVE THIS RIDDLE: WHAT AM I? I AM A RIVER THAT CARRIES TWO BOATS, ONE BY NIGHT AND ONE BY DAY. I CLOSE MY MOUTH AND IT IS NIGHT. I OPEN IT AND IT IS DAY. MY FEET AND HANDS NEVER LEAVE THE EARTH, BUT I AM HIGH ABOVE IT. I ROLL A BALL ON MY STOMACH AND WEAR SPANGLES ON MY BODY. SAY NOW, WHAT AM I?"

"What do we do?" Amy said. "What's happening to us? I'm scared."

"We must answer the riddle," Harry told her.

"This is unreal!" Josh said.

"No it isn't," Harry said. "It's real—in fact, it's better than real."

"ANSWER MY RIDDLE!" The bird-woman flapped her wings threateningly. "QUICKLY, OR I WILL ATTACK!"

8

Death of a Princess

The bird-woman towered over them. She turned her cruel-beaked face to one side to regard them with a single threatening painted eye. Would she pounce if they failed her test? She had brought the whiff of carrion with her, Josh noticed. Amy wrinkled her nose.

"I know the answer," Harry said.

"So do I," Amy said.

Josh's mind was a blank. Why were these questions so cryptic? "But it's my turn," he said. "Let me try this one."

"You've got to keep your eyes open as you go through the game," Amy told him. "You've got to notice things along the way, even things that don't seem important, and you've got to listen to things that are said—even by us. We keep on giving each other clues, it seems. Nothing is outside of this game. It's listening to us."

Josh scowled. Was he dumb? Maybe Amy was right. He'd have to start noticing things a bit more.

"We saw the answer to this riddle in the first chamber," Amy said.

"Now you're giving me clues," Josh said peevishly. "You sound like one of those stupid boxes on the screen."

"It was in the burial chamber," Amy prompted him again. "Think about what you saw."

Josh was still puzzled. "Isis?"

"No," Harry said. "But things are looking up."

Looking up? Another clue.

"Don't give it to me!" Josh felt himself colouring with embarrassment and anger. They were treating him like an idiot.

"This is stupid, Josh," Amy said anxiously. "That thing could pounce on us. Let somebody else answer the riddle if you can't."

"No. I want this turn! I got the last answer right."

"You're putting us in danger," Harry said. "There's a time limit. If we fail—I don't know what will happen. Maybe the same thing that happened to Spy."

"Come on, Josh. Picture the burial chamber," Amy encouraged him. "You have to remember every bit of the game."

Josh turned his mind back. What was he looking for? Why hadn't he paid more attention? *Think. What did you see?* His memory of the chamber was a blank. Then details began to form. He pictured the vault of stars, gods and goddesses. He remembered the figure that Amy had admired, the golden girl arched over all, a goddess with her hands and feet touching the earth. The sun wheeled through her body at night to be born in the morning, and stars spangled her body ...

"The answer is Nut, the sky goddess," Josh said.

The bird-woman flapped her wings as if ready to pounce.

Oh, no, Josh thought. *Maybe I'm wrong.* He took a

65

step back.

The bird-woman cawed. "THAT IS THE CORRECT ANSWER. YOU HAVE SECURED THE SECOND LEG OF OSIRIS. GO ON TO THE NEXT CHALLENGE: TO FIND THE ARM OF OSIRIS."

She flew up in a swirl of feathers and took off into the darkness at the top of the cage, departing so swiftly that her going made a vacuum that tugged at their hair.

"Good one, Josh," Harry said, relieved.

"It took you long enough," Amy said edgily. "If you had noticed the tomb painting the way I did, you'd have remembered it more easily."

"At least he got it," Harry said.

The leg vanished, and so did the cage, but the room did not return. The three found themselves once again running along a stone passage.

I haven't really solved anything on my own yet, Josh thought. I'd better do something good pretty soon—or give up. I'm making an idiot of myself.

Why was he finding it so hard? Normally he had no difficulty with computer games. Maybe it was because this was no normal computer game. Was he really running along these passages and facing challenges? Or was it some trick of the game? Had it gripped his attention so completely that he merely thought he was caught up in it?

Without warning, they left the passage and stepped into a brightly lit bedchamber.

A young woman wearing a fine white pleated gown lay motionless on a leopard-headed couch. On her head was the golden circlet of a princess. A handmaiden knelt weeping beside her, bobbing up and down in grief. Once again the players heard the tremulous eastern wail of lament.

What was happening here? Where were they? Josh examined the bedchamber. It was richly furnished. As well as the ornate leopard-headed couch, there were finely decorated chests, tables piled with food and drink, inlaid chairs, colourful hangings and mats. A cat lay cleaning itself on a floor that was decorated with a pattern of waterlilies and blue wavy lines like ripples.

At the sight of the cat, Amy gave a wail. "I'd nearly forgotten poor Spy! Where is he? Give him back to me, you horrible game."

"Careful," Harry said. "You know it's touchy."

The arm of Osiris lay on a table.

A man with the feathered head, curved beak and flashing eyes of an eagle stepped into the chamber. His voice was like the cry of an eagle.

"TO RECOVER THE FIRST ARM OF OSIRIS, YOU MUST SOLVE THE MYSTERY OF AN UNTIMELY DEATH. THE YOUNG PRINCESS TETISHERY LIES DEAD ON HER COUCH. HOW DID SHE DIE? ONE CLUE: THE PRINCESS SAW THE AGENT OF HER DEATH REFLECTED IN HER HAND-MIRROR. I WILL BE YOUR REFEREE. IN THIS SECTION OF THE GAME YOU MAY POINT TO AN OBJECT IF YOU REQUIRE GENERAL INFORMATION. HOWEVER, IF YOU BELIEVE YOU HAVE THE RIGHT ANSWER, YOU MUST TOUCH THE OBJECT. HURRY! IF YOU FAIL, YOU WILL NEVER GO BACK!"

"A murder mystery," Amy said. "Start looking around

the room, Josh. We have to look for clues."

"Don't tell me what to do," Josh said. "I deserve first go again. I got the last answer right."

"With a bit of help."

Where should they start looking? If the princess saw her killer in her hand-mirror, then he might have been sneaking up behind her. Was he still hiding somewhere in the chamber? Under the bed?

Josh pointed at the leopard-headed couch. The bird-man spoke again:

"THAT IS AN EGYPTIAN ROYAL COUCH WITH LEOPARD-HEADED MOUNTS AND FEET WITH CLAWS OF GOLD. EGYPTIAN BEDS SLOPED FROM HEAD TO FOOT. INSTEAD OF A PILLOW, THE ANCIENT EGYPTIANS USED A HARD HEADREST, ON WHICH WAS PLACED A SMALL CUSHION FOR COMFORT."

Not much help.

"There's food on the table," Harry said.

Josh went to the table and pointed. The bird-man responded:

"THE PRINCESS TETISHERY DINED ON FRESHLY BAKED BREAD AND BABY CHICKEN ROASTED IN HONEY. SHE FOLLOWED THIS WITH A SELECTION OF FRUIT—GRAPES, DATES, FIGS AND POMEGRANATES. IF YOU BELIEVE THIS WAS THE CAUSE OF HER DEATH, TOUCH THE FOOD."

"Aha," Josh said. "She was poisoned!"

"A bit too obvious," Amy said sceptically.

"I agree," Harry said. "Besides, Egyptian royalty had special tasters who tasted their food before they ate it. They couldn't run the risk of being poisoned by a rival."

"That's your opinion," Josh said, feeling irritated.

Didn't they think he could solve it? They were taking over again.

"We're all in this together," Harry reminded him.

"Yeah, well, you could both be wrong," Josh said belligerently. He was growing tired of failing in their eyes. "The taster couldn't have tasted every single grape."

"Don't touch the food, Josh."

Josh shrugged. "There's a jug of wine on another table—and a goblet. I'll try that. Maybe she drank some poison." He pointed.

"THE PRINCESS TETISHERY DRANK A GLASS OF FINE WINE WITH HER MEAL. EGYPTIANS MADE A VARIETY OF WINES AND BEER."

"Same story as the food," Harry said. "A taster would have tasted the wine, too."

"Let's have a look at her cosmetics box, Josh," Amy said.

Not that again. Josh sighed wearily. He mustn't let Amy get stuck on make-up. They were trying to solve a murder mystery.

"Later," he said. He had noticed a large decorated chest in the bedchamber. Perhaps the murderer was hiding inside it? It looked big enough. He pointed to it. The bird-man gave an explanation:

"THAT IS A DECORATED CHEST. EGYPTIANS DID NOT HAVE WARDROBES OR CLOSETS, AND STORED THEIR POSSESSIONS IN CHESTS OF VARYING SIZE AND DESIGN. THEY COULD CONTAIN ANYTHING FROM CLOTHING AND PERSONAL EFFECTS TO THE TREASURES OF A KING."

"I want to see what's inside the cosmetics box," Amy repeated.

"Amy," Josh said with exaggerated patience, "you already know what's inside a cosmetics box. The same things we saw last time."

"All the same, I want to see."

"Okay," Josh said grudgingly. He pointed to the box. "THAT IS AN ORNAMENTAL WOODEN COSMETICS BOX. INSIDE IS A MIRROR, A COMB, EYE MAKE-UP AND COSMETICS, PERFUMES AND UNGUENTS ..."

"See? The same old stuff again," Josh complained.

"I want to see *inside*," Amy insisted. "Remember the clue. The princess saw something in her hand-mirror, so she was probably putting on her make-up at the time."

"I know, I know. I was working my way towards that," Josh said.

He pointed to the box again, and now it flipped open magically to reveal its contents. It looked even messier than the bottom of their mother's make-up drawer. A jar of eyeliner had fallen over, lost its lid and spilt, leaving dry, caked stains on the bottom of the box.

Josh looked up at the bird-man. The eagle eyes flashed.

The polished bronze hand-mirror caught Josh's attention. He remembered the words of the eagle-headed guardian: "*The princess saw the agent of her death reflected in her hand-mirror.*"

Amy was solving the puzzle. He must beat her to it.

"She looked into her hand-mirror and saw the killer," Josh announced triumphantly. "The answer's obvious."

He saw it now. The truth hit him with a flash, like a mirror catching light. The princess had seen the reflection of her own face. She had killed herself. It wasn't murder, but suicide.

"What would a princess have seen when she looked into her hand-mirror but herself ... her own face!" he said.

"Close," Amy said. "But wrong."

Wrong? Josh scowled at her.

What else could the princess have seen?

9

The Chariot Race

"She didn't just see her face," Amy said. "She saw her *made-up* face. Think about the make-up. See how messy her cosmetics box is? See how her eyeliner has tipped over, and all the liquid has spilt out and dried up?"

"Yes, but what does that prove?" Harry said.

"Don't you see? Somebody deliberately spilt her eyeliner and left the lid off," Amy said.

"But why?"

"Because they knew what she would do if she found that her eyeliner had dried up. What does Mum do when her eyeliner goes a bit dry?"

"She buys a new one," Harry ventured.

"Eventually, but what does she do at the time?"

"I don't know."

"The natural thing to do is to wet it with your tongue. You lick the brush, put some eye-liner on, lick it again. Get it? Poison. The dried-up eyeliner was laced with poison, probably a slow-acting poison that would only work after her meal. I'll bet the handmaiden poisoned it. Remember the clue: *The princess saw the agent of her death reflected in her hand-mirror.* The princess probably saw two things while she was busy using her mirror: the make-up going on her face and the hand-maiden standing behind her doing her hair. It's one of those Egyptian puns. The word 'agent' means both the poison—the chemical agent of her death—and the handmaiden—the human agent who put it there."

"That's what I was trying to explain all the time," Josh heard himself say. "The princess looked into the mirror and saw herself—and her make-up. Obviously she had make-up on her face. I didn't need to say that, did I?"

To prevent Amy from taking over, he gingerly picked up the bottle of eye make-up, careful to touch only the clean surface. "Here is the instrument of her death."

The eagle-headed man bowed. "WELL DONE. YOU HAVE SOLVED THE MYSTERY OF THE MURDER OF PRINCESS TETISHERY. YOU HAVE NOW RECOVERED THE FIRST ARM OF OSIRIS."

The bird-man vanished in a flash, and the arm of Osiris disappeared off the table.

Josh dropped the bottle back into the cosmetics box.

Amy rounded on him. "Are you trying to tell us *you* thought of it?" she said. "Tell the truth. Admit you had no idea of the answer."

It was hard to bluff those clear grey eyes. "Of course I knew!"

"You just won't give me credit, will you?" she blazed. "You're as bad as Mum. Nobody will give me credit for anything I do!"

Josh flushed. He thought of admitting his failure, then caught the look of disappointment in Harry's eyes and decided against it. Maybe later.

The bedchamber vanished, and the three found themselves on the move again, running along another passage. Josh felt tired. He was breathing heavily. His feet hurt from pounding along the hard stone floor.

They moved on, and turned a corner. The dimness of the passage exploded into light as a blinding sunlit scene opened up around them. They had come into a vast, oval-shaped arena filled with hard-baked sand. A rumbling roar rose from the throats of the crowd gathered around the oval.

The second mummified arm of Osiris lay under the shade of a canopy in a small pavilion. Two chariots, each hitched to a pair of stamping horses, stood on the track. One was empty. In the other stood a pharaoh wearing the glittering royal war crown.

A bald-headed man dressed in white appeared at the edge of the track. He seemed to be some kind of official, for he wore a jewelled collar that winked in the sunshine as he spoke:

"TO SECURE THE SECOND ARM OF OSIRIS, YOU MUST DEFEAT THE PHARAOH RAMESES IN A CHARIOT RACE. YOU MUST RACE THREE TIMES AROUND THE TRACK. THE FIRST CHARIOTEER ACROSS THE FINISH LINE IS THE WINNER."

"Great, some action!" Harry said enthusiastically. "I wish it was my turn."

"Well, it's not," Josh said, gaining new interest. This was more like it! He was glad now that he hadn't admitted that Amy had solved the last challenge. He could still claim that it was *his* turn.

Josh liked to race. It called for a good eye and swift reflexes, skills that had made him the school champion at a computer game called Grand Prix Circuit. But this wasn't a computer race. These were real horses. He could smell them.

"CLIMB INTO YOUR CHARIOT," the official said.

"Go on, do it," Harry said. "Or I will."

Josh walked out across the sand towards the chariot. Amy and Harry stayed at the edge of the track.

When he reached it, Josh eyed the two-wheeled, lightweight chariot in amazement. It was little bigger than the sort of rig used in harness racing, except that it had a platform on which the driver could stand. The horses reared and whinnied, quivering with excitement and sweating as if they had been exercised. Josh climbed aboard the chariot and took hold of the leather reins.

The pharaoh in the other chariot looked real, but he had gleaming electronic eyes. His eyes flashed at Josh as if he were confident of a secret superiority, certain of victory.

The bald-headed official came out on to the track, raised a white cloth in the air and dropped it.

Josh flicked the reins. His twin chargers reared up on their hind legs and then took off with a rumble of hoofs.

He'd left Rameses standing. His hair streamed in the breeze and his shirt fluttered. He felt as if he was riding his skateboard. Dust billowed behind him.

They were coming into a turn. Josh knew not to take it wide, or he'd lose valuable time. He drew on the reins and brought the chariot smoothly around the curve and out into the straight.

"Look behind you, Josh!" Amy screamed.

"So Rameses is coming, so what? Let him eat my dust," Josh called out over his shoulder. But as he glanced back at the pursuing chariot, he realised that it wasn't Rameses he had to worry about. It was the bow and arrow in the pharaoh's hands.

No wonder Rameses had looked so confident. He had weapons to ensure his victory.

Wrapping the reins around one arm, the pharaoh bent his bow, drawing the fletching of the arrow to the anchor point at his chin.

Josh waited until the bow snapped straight, then ducked low. The arrow buzzed harmlessly overhead.

Josh turned his mind back to the race. He had lost valuable speed, and Rameses was closing on him. He had to slow down now as he neared another bend. He guided his two galloping horses into the corner. A bit wide. *That'll cost me time*. He glanced back at Rameses. The pharaoh's chariot slid smoothly around the bend.

Josh was back in the straight, rushing towards Harry and Amy, who were jumping up and down in excitement.

He glanced behind him again. Rameses had put down the bow. Now he was close enough to use a spear. He held it high over his shining war crown, ready to launch it.

"Duck!" Harry yelled.

Josh crouched. The spear whizzed overhead so low it almost parted his hair, but he was still alive. He jumped up again to find that his chariot was straying hopelessly off course. It was perhaps just as well. Rameses' second spear went wide.

Josh lurched around the bend and into the straight.

Rameses did not go wide at the corner. He cut it finely. Now he was close enough to use a sword.

Josh flicked the reins over the horses' backs to speed them on. He pulled ahead fractionally. Rameses was trying to take the corner on the inside. *No you don't. I won't leave you enough track.* Josh swung his horses into the bend, taking it tightly. Too tightly.

Disaster!

The chariot turned over and Josh flew into the air. He landed on the sandy track, falling hard.

Amazingly, the chariot righted itself, but the horses slowed without their driver. Rameses was closing in for the kill, his sword arm raised.

"Get up!" Harry shouted.

Josh got up and ran after his chariot. *Wait for me!* he willed the horses. His heart was thudding as loudly as his pounding feet. Rameses was right behind him. Josh leaped back on to the driving platform.

Rameses flashed by, swinging his sword. Josh ducked. Now Rameses had hit the front, passing Amy and Harry at the side of the track. Josh took off in pursuit. This was the last lap.

Just as he reached the next bend, Rameses twisted in his chariot to see how Josh was doing. The distraction made him take the corner wide. Josh did not make the same mistake, but hugged the bend to close the gap.

When they went into the straight again, Rameses reached for his bow. He took aim, and the arrow flew.

Josh bobbed down, and it missed. Rameses had lost more speed.

Rameses put down the bow and reached for his sword. While he did that, Josh drew level. Rameses leaned out of his chariot with the sword in his hand, and instinctively Josh ducked. If he hadn't ducked, he might have seen that Rameses was not swinging the sword at him, but at the harness of the horses.

The blade sliced through the leather straps, and Josh's horses broke free. The chariot crashed to the ground, skidding like a stone to a stop. Josh's horses pulled up and Rameses reined in too. Then he turned his chariot around and drove back to the sprawled figure of his rival.

"Sorry, guys, I've done it this time," Josh called out in despair.

Rameses came closer, his eyes flashing triumphantly.

"Don't give up, Josh!" Harry called. "There's something you can do that Rameses would never expect. See where your horses are. You can *ride* to the finish! Egyptian nobles never rode on the backs of horses. They were too stuck-up. You can give him a surprise."

Josh scrambled to his feet. He ran past the pharaoh's chariot to his waiting horses, who were standing at the edge of the track, still tethered together. He sprang on to the back of the nearest one. The animal reared in surprise, but Josh clung on. The horses bolted around the corner and into the straight.

10

The Head of Osiris

Arrows whizzed past Josh's head, but he kept going. When he crossed the finish line, there was a roar from the crowd, and loud cheers from Amy and Harry.

Rameses pulled up in his chariot, his electronic eyes shooting sparks of anger. He climbed down from his chariot, took off the war crown and jumped on it in rage. Then he and the entire scene disappeared in a burst of light.

The track had gone. They were back in a passageway.

Josh had won the second arm of Osiris. Now for the head.

Harry patted him on the back. "Great race, Josh!"

"Well done." Amy added her congratulations, but a bit grudgingly, Josh thought.

He had beaten Rameses! Josh felt exhilarated, yet something nagged at him. The others had helped him again. Amy had alerted him to Rameses' sly bow and arrow attack. Harry had suggested that he finish the race on horseback.

Josh made an effort to sharpen his thinking. It was about time he did something to impress the others.

On his own.

Involuntarily they broke into a run, drawn by a force that pulled them onwards.

"Look what's coming, Josh!"

A mummified mouse streaked down the passage towards them, followed by a yowling, spitting mummy cat. They swerved out of its way.

"What a horrible cat," Amy said. "Not like my lovely Spy."

"It's horrible to us, but to the ancient Egyptians it was sacred," Harry explained. "Killing a cat was a crime punishable by death. Cats were so precious that if a house was on fire, Egyptians would rescue their cat before anything else."

"Egyptians aren't the only ones who think cats are precious!" Amy said angrily. "Spy is very precious to me, and I want him back!"

"Look ahead!"

Down the passage came another bandaged yowler, bounding after a scurrying mummy mouse. Josh, Amy and Harry dodged. The cat sprang at them, and they threw themselves against a wall so hard that they fell to the floor. The cat flashed past, spitting with rage.

They picked themselves up and ran on.

Josh felt his fight coming back. He sent a silent message to the game: *Give me a chance and I'll show you. Give me your toughest problem and I'll solve it.*

"I'm getting tired," Amy complained. "I need a break. Can't we get out of this game now?"

"The game doesn't want to let us out yet," Harry said. "It's pulling us along."

"Who wants to stop?" Josh said. "I'm just getting into it!"

They ran into a tomb stocked with tomb furniture.

As they entered the chamber they were startled by a grating sound behind them. A heavy stone portcullis rumbled to the floor.

"We're trapped," Harry shouted.

A huge man with a black jackal's head stepped out of the shadows and snarled at them: "I AM ANUBIS, LORD OF THE MUMMY WRAPPINGS, INVENTOR OF THE MORTUARY RITES. THE HEAD OF OSIRIS IS HIDDEN IN THIS SEALED TOMB. ONE OF THE TOMB OBJECTS CONTAINS THE INFORMATION YOU SEEK. YOU MAY ASK QUESTIONS ABOUT ANY OBJECT, BUT YOU MAY OPEN ONLY ONE. A CLUE: DO NOT TAKE THINGS AT FACE VALUE. LOOK BELOW THE SURFACE. IF YOU CANNOT FIND THE HEAD OF OSIRIS, YOU WILL REMAIN HERE FOREVER AND YOU WILL FAIL IN YOUR QUEST. PLAY, AND BE SWIFT!"

"How do you ask questions?" Amy said.

"POINT TO AN OBJECT," the jackal-headed one said, "AND THEN I WILL TELL YOU ABOUT IT. IF YOU WANT TO OPEN SOMETHING, SIMPLY REQUEST THAT IT BE OPENED. BUT REMEMBER, YOU ARE ALLOWED TO OPEN ONLY ONE THING."

"Um," Josh said thoughtfully. It was still his turn: he had won the chariot race, even though the others had helped him. He still wanted to prove himself.

He studied the objects in the tomb. Four large jars with unusual stoppers caught his eye. The first jar had the head of a baboon, the second a dog's head, the third a human head, the last the head of a falcon.

Josh pointed to the jars, and Anubis snarled his answer.

"THESE ARE CALLED CANOPIC JARS. WHEN ANCIENT EGYPTIANS WERE MUMMIFIED, THEIR INTERNALS— LIVER, LUNGS, STOMACH AND INTESTINES—WERE REMOVED AND PLACED IN THESE FOUR JARS. THE INTERNALS WERE THOUGHT TO BE UNDER THE PROTECTION OF FOUR INDIVIDUAL GUARDIANS, THE SONS OF HORUS: HAPI—BABOON-HEADED; AMSET— HUMAN-HEADED; DUAMUTEF—DOG-HEADED; QEBEHSENUF— FALCON-HEADED."

Not much help. Josh's eyes went next to a wooden coffin. The lid had been drawn back and a shiny painted mask moved aside to reveal the wrapped head of a mummy. Was this the head of Osiris?

He pointed in the direction of the mummy's head. Anubis thought he was pointing at the mask, a human face with staring painted eyes.

"THE MUMMY MASK CUSTOMARILY PLACED OVER THE MUMMY'S FACE WAS FASHIONED IN THE LIKENESS OF THE DEAD—"

"Not that ..."

Too late. Josh felt a flash of annoyance as Anubis explained about the wrong thing. He squirmed impatiently.

"... THE MOST FAMOUS EXAMPLE IS THE GOLDEN MUMMY MASK OF TUTANKHAMUN. EXQUISITELY MADE AND POLISHED, IT WEIGHS ALMOST ELEVEN KILOGRAMS. BUT NOT ALL MUMMY MASKS WERE SO GRAND. MANY MASKS WERE MERELY MADE OF CARTONNAGE—SHEETS

OF LINEN STIFFENED WITH PLASTER. SOMETIMES STRIPS OF OLD PAPYRUS WERE USED. SOME LOST TEXTS HAVE COME TO LIGHT WHEN THESE WERE EXAMINED ..."

"That's interesting," Amy said. "I wonder what that one's made of? It doesn't look like gold."

Josh didn't find it interesting. There was nothing more annoying than having to listen to a boring lesson on something he didn't want to know about. This wasn't helping him to find the head of Osiris.

He went closer and this time almost stabbed the mummy with his finger to make his intention clear.

"A MUMMY," responded Anubis. "THE WORD 'MUMMY' COMES FROM THE PERSIAN WORD 'MOUMIA', MEANING BITUMEN. BECAUSE OF THEIR OFTEN BLACK-ENED APPEARANCE, MUMMIES WERE THOUGHT TO BE IMPREGNATED WITH BITUMEN. FOR THIS REASON THEY WERE BELIEVED TO HAVE MEDICINAL USE AND A BRISK TRADE IN 'MUMMY' EXISTED IN THE MIDDLE AGES. THE PROCESS OF MUMMIFICATION BEGAN WHEN A BODY WAS EMBALMED IN DRY NATRON AND VARIOUS SPICES FOR SEVENTY DAYS. DURING THIS TIME THE MUMMY LOST AT LEAST SEVENTY-FIVE PER CENT OF ITS BODY WEIGHT. THE MUMMY WAS WRAPPED IN HUNDREDS OF METRES OF FINE LINEN WITH MANY SACRED AMULETS BOUND INTO THE FOLDS. THE MOST IMPORTANT OF THESE WAS A SCARAB BEETLE JEWEL, SYMBOLISING AND PROTECTING THE HEART. EGYPTIANS BELIEVED THAT IN ORDER TO ENJOY AN AFTERLIFE, THE BODY MUST BE PRESERVED AS A HOME FOR THE SOUL. THE SOUL COULD JOURNEY IN HEAVEN, VISIT OLD HAUNTS ON EARTH OR DWELL IN THE TOMB IN THE FORM OF A SOUL BIRD."

No good, thought Josh. Blast. He'd slow down, think more carefully.

"Take your time," Harry said. "But not too long. We don't know how much time we're allowed for each challenge."

"Thanks, Harry," Josh muttered under his breath.

He stared at the tomb furniture. There were gaming boards, a painted chest, a model of a boat with a deck-house on top, another large chest covered in gold leaf. Maybe he'd ask about that. Then there was a large wooden shrine resting on a sledge.

He pointed out the shrine. The jackal growled.

"THIS LARGE SHRINE, DECORATED WITH FINE GOLD LEAF, IS MADE IN THE SHAPE OF A PAVILION. IT RESTS ON A SLEDGE, AND BY CUSTOM IT WAS DRAGGED TO THE TOMB."

Josh scratched his chin. Should he ask Anubis to open the shrine? What about pointing to the painted chest, instead? *Do it*, he told himself. *Solve it before the other two start giving you helpful clues, or worse, solve it for you.* Harry and Amy were showing him up. He'd never be able to face them again if he didn't crack this one.

Probably he'd been given a clue earlier, but how was he supposed to remember everything? This was worse than a history lesson. He didn't want to be fed all this stuff. If he was wrong, tough.

He felt the others' eyes on him. Amy was giving him a warning stare. "Be careful, Josh," she said. "Don't be in such a hurry to succeed that you ruin everything."

"Yeah," Harry said. "It doesn't matter who thinks of the answer first. Don't try to come up with something just because you think it's your go. We have to play this game together."

They were counting on him, trusting him not to be reckless.

Josh thought of Isis bobbing up and down in the burial chamber, tears streaming from her eyes. She was counting on him too.

Then there was Spy, running lost and alone somewhere in the darkness.

Josh's shoulders slumped. Amy and Harry were right. His attitude was a danger to them all.

11

Taking an Interest

Suddenly Josh realised that he was thinking about this game in the wrong way. He remembered how, the first time they had played the game, Amy had solved the problem of the doorway. She had solved it *because she had taken an interest*. She had remembered something Harry had said about coffins also being houses of eternity.

He recalled the clue they had been given: *Do not take things at face value. Look below the surface.*

Face value. Below the surface. His mind was blank. What had interested him about the information he had heard? Not much. He remembered squirming with impatience as the jackal-headed Anubis had explained about the mummy mask, answering a question he hadn't meant to ask. Then a glimmer of light came up on the dark horizon of his mind. What was it? A small fact, a gleam of interest ... He remembered something Anubis had said: "... *Many masks were merely made of cartonnage—sheets of linen stiffened with plaster. Sometimes strips of old papyrus were used. Some lost texts have come to light when these were examined ...*"

"I'm going to try something," Josh said.

"Careful," Harry warned him.

"I think I know where to find the answer."

Josh went over to the mummy mask.

"What are you doing, Josh?" Harry said. "You've already asked a question about the mummy mask."

"I know. But remember the clue? We shouldn't take things at face value. I want to look below the surface."

Josh heard Amy's sharp intake of breath.

"No!" Harry yelled.

"Open the mummy mask," Josh said.

The cartonnage mask peeled back as if ripped by invisible hands. The painted layers came off. But there was something beneath them—brown, textured material. It was papyrus. There was writing on it.

Anubis snapped his jaws together. "VERY CLEVER. THE ANSWER TO THE PUZZLE IS HIDDEN IN THE LAYERS OF PAPYRUS BENEATH THE SURFACE OF THE MASK. READ WHAT IS WRITTEN ON THE PAPYRUS."

Josh bent over the mask. As he looked at the mysterious hieroglyphic characters on the papyrus, the words came effortlessly to his mind.

"The head of Osiris is concealed at the feet of the mummy," he read aloud.

Now the partly drawn back lid of the coffin came back all the way, and there was the mummified head of Osiris, sitting like a football at the mummy's feet. One eye was missing.

"Good one, Josh," Harry said, his voice cracking with relief.

Amy looked impressed.

Josh was past appreciating their approval. His hands were trembling. But he'd done it.

The head vanished.

The giant Anubis with the black jackal's head bared his teeth. "GOOD WORK," he growled. "NOW YOU MUST GO ON TO FIND THE INTERNAL ORGANS OF OSIRIS. THEY ARE HIDDEN TOGETHER, GUARDED BY THE FOUR SONS OF HORUS. HURRY."

As if to remind them of their goal, they heard the faraway sound of Isis wailing. The wails seemed even more spirit-wrenching than before.

"Stop!" Amy said, blocking her ears with her hands. "I can't stand that crying."

As he led the others along the passage, Josh felt the warmth of victory. He was getting the feel of this game now. He had shown them what he could do when he put his mind to it—when he took an interest.

"I thought we were finished back there," Harry confessed. "But you solved it, Josh." There was a bit more respect in his voice now.

He's not such a bad kid, Josh thought.

"Listen to that," Amy said, clutching Josh's arm.

A cat was yowling somewhere in the darkness.

"Is that Spy?" Harry asked hopefully.

"Spy doesn't sound like that," Amy answered.

"Let's keep going," Josh said.

The passage took them to another chamber, empty except for four large canopic jars. They looked around. The chamber was brightly lit by flickering wall torches. There was nothing else in the room. No guardian this time. The jars looked like four large, dumpy salt and pepper shakers with carved heads on top in the images of a human, a baboon, a falcon and a jackal.

"This is easy," Josh said. "The guards must have knocked off."

The human head on one of the jars shook from side to side, refuting this statement. The baboon head and the jackal head snarled, flashing their teeth. The falcon head lunged at them with its beak.

Josh drew back swiftly.

"WE ARE THE SONS OF HORUS: HAPI, THE BABOON-HEADED; AMSET, THE HUMAN-HEADED; DUAMUTEF, THE DOG-HEADED; AND QEBEHSENUF, THE FALCON-HEADED, GUARDIANS OF THE CANOPIC JARS. TO REGAIN THE ORGANS OF OSIRIS, YOU MUST FIRST ANSWER THIS RIDDLE: WHAT AM I? I WAS BORN IN SEVENTY DAYS. THOUGH TREATED WITH COSTLY BALM, I COULD NOT BE CURED. IN DEATH I WAS SOUGHT AS A HEALER OF THE SICK. MY FAME SPREAD FAR AND WIDE: ONCE A PERISHED ONE, NOW A PHYSICIAN, DYING TO HEAL THE BRUISED."

Josh thought hard. It didn't make sense. Did the riddle refer to some famous Egyptian physician? This was Harry's territory. It was probably time he gave Harry a turn. He, Josh, had shown his skills now. He turned to Harry. "Know any Egyptian doctors?"

"There was Imhotep, the father of Egyptian medicine, who became the god of physicians after his death. Maybe ... but I don't think that's the answer." He looked thoughtfully at Amy.

"Don't look at me, Harry. I haven't a clue."

"Try Imhotep," Josh said.

"No, I don't think so," Harry said. "The answer is a mummy."

"A mummy?"

"Don't you remember, mummies were born or embalmed in seventy days, and in the Middle Ages people thought they contained medicinal properties. Mummy was ground up and taken as medicine to cure bruises and stomach upsets—"

"Yuk!" Amy said.

"Look at the jars."

The four heads on the canopic jars dipped in a bow. The baboon-headed one chattered. "YOU HAVE SOLVED THE PUZZLE OF THE SONS OF HORUS. YOUR NEXT CHALLENGE IS TO FIND THE BODY OF OSIRIS. IT IS GUARDED BY GHOSTS CALLED PHARAOH PHANTOMS."

The faraway sound of a tooting horn startled the children. They heard the engine, the crunch of tyres on gravel as a car pulled into the driveway.

"Mum's home!" Amy said.

How could they hear a car here in the chamber? Josh was surprised that a sound from the real world could reach them. He felt as if they had travelled a vast distance from his bedroom. Was it merely an illusion?

They turned around. The chamber had vanished. They saw lines running out of the passage and back to Josh's bedroom. The bedroom looked tiny, as though seen through the wrong end of a telescope.

"We'd better stop playing and get back!" Josh said. "Or Mum's going to go crook at me."

"But we still don't have Spy!"

"And we've only got the body, the eye and the heart

of Osiris to go," Harry pleaded.

"Tomorrow," Josh said.

They turned and raced back, following the pulsating lines. It seemed that the passage stretched endlessly, and yet the car engine was still running when they spilled out of the darkness and into the familiar surroundings of Josh's bedroom.

12

The Body of Osiris

"Will you take Tina for a walk, Josh?"

"Sorry, Aunt Helen," Harry said. "I forgot to remind him."

Their mother cooked dinner while Harry and Amy set the table.

Josh took the poodle by her lead and collected his skateboard from the garage. He was glad to get out of the house. He jumped on the board and rode it down the slope of the driveway and along the pavement, the urethane wheels bumping pleasantly beneath the soles of his sneakers. Tina ran happily behind him.

It was a hot, sticky evening, with no cool breeze. The humidity pressed like a warm, damp cloth on Josh's face. He felt that the run of the skateboard wheels no longer led his thoughts in a clear line. He seemed to be teetering, not quite co-ordinated.

He put on more speed.

The new kid on the block appeared on a skateboard ahead of him and grinned playfully at Josh over his shoulder. Obviously he'd decided that if he couldn't join Josh, he'd play his game and try to beat him. He put out his leg and paddled furiously, using the traction of a pair of sneakers that had deep lugged soles like tractor tyres. To block Josh and stop him passing, he threw the board into a snaking line.

Stupid kid. Josh snatched up Tina in his arms and bent low, powering after the boy. He sailed inside the curves described by the boy's skateboard, going extra close to give him a scare, and flicked past him. The boy came off his board and rolled on to the grassy verge.

Serves him right. Josh was feeling mad. The Mummy Monster Game was getting to him.

He was caught in a bind. On the one hand, he knew the risk he was taking: if his mother caught him playing on the computer instead of doing his homework, he would be banned from the computer for a week. On the other hand, they needed to finish the game—and the longer they took to complete their quest, the greater the danger. What else might come through into their own world?

He hoped the kid on the skateboard hadn't hurt himself, and looked regretfully over his shoulder to check. The boy was okay, but he'd lost his fight. He was skating home in the other direction.

Poor kid. He seemed lonely. I shouldn't have taken it out on him, Josh thought.

Crossing the street, he turned into the parklands and put Tina on the ground. Shadows were gathering among the trees. The park lights that illuminated the pathways hadn't come on yet.

He chose a smooth concrete path with a downward slope that gave extra speed to his wheels. Tina bounded behind him. The little dog could run like a hare.

Josh wondered what to do. Should he continue to play the computer game alone, secretly, overnight? No—too risky, for a number of reasons. Too scary for a start. But also dangerous in another sense. What if his mother caught him and confiscated the computer, as she had threatened to do? That didn't bear thinking about. He'd just have to ride it out.

Tina gave a yelp behind him.

"What's the matter, girl?"

Josh twisted on the board. Tina was still running, in fact running even faster, but she was throwing anxious glances behind her at a row of gum trees. Josh saw a giant shadow separate itself from the rest and he thought he glimpsed, in silhouette, the figure of a man with something on his head—a long object. The head turned to look at him. A picture of the mummy monster with the long crocodile jaws reared in Josh's memory.

He froze, balancing on the skateboard.

Tina jumped up against his leg, and he scooped her into his arms.

"What is it, girl?"

Not crocodile head, surely?

Now that she was safely tucked in Josh's arms, Tina growled deep in her throat. Josh wondered if he should go back to look, then changed his mind. He'd better get home.

As he scooted on, he thought he heard movement behind him, pounding feet. Was the monster chasing him?

Let's see how you go against my skateboard, he thought.

He turned into the road that ran through the park,

careering along it. He dared a backward glance. A shadow was moving through the trees. Josh forgot about the speed humps in the middle of the road. He hit one hard, and he and his board parted company.

Luckily, it was a trick he was used to doing. He managed to land back on the board, but none too squarely, and he teetered dangerously. Tina, afraid of falling, struggled in his arms. Josh steadied and kicked himself along faster. He hit full speed and turned into another downward slope. Nothing would catch him now.

He left the park through the gateway, crossed the street to the far pavement and followed the pavement around the block, skating for home. Although he was shaking inside, he felt strengthened and sharpened by the encounter. He had beaten that thing in the park, whatever it was.

He put Tina down and climbed a rise, working hard. At the top of the rise, he straightened and allowed himself an easy glide down the other side. Harry was telling the truth about the game. Bigger and scarier things *were* coming through.

The four rolling wheels under the board brought his jangled thoughts back into line. What would he tell the others? Could he be sure about what he'd seen? Maybe the game was spooking him.

Josh's mother and Tina the poodle woke him up the next morning.

"Don't be late again, Josh. If you get up now you can beat your sister to the shower."

Tina licked his nose. Josh opened one eye. "Thanks,

Mum," he said.

He jumped out of bed straight away, and his mother left the room. Tina ran to his wardrobe, sniffed at the door, and pawed at it.

"Out, Tina," Josh said, chasing her.

When he came out of his shower, his mother was standing in front of the wardrobe—*and the door was open*!

"What are you doing in my wardrobe, Mum?" he said, anxiously.

"Josh, this is a horrible mess! I told you to tidy it up—it looks like a junk yard! Will you never listen to me? You're driving me crazy!" she blurted, hardly pausing between the words, the way she did when she was on the war path. She seemed to be doing it a lot lately. "Look at this stuff!"

She dipped into the wardrobe and hauled out two footballs, an old rugby ball and then a dingy white lump of fabric. Josh felt a nudge under his heart. From the corner of his eye, it looked like the round, bandaged head of a mummy.

The head rolled on to the carpet. No, it was only a towel. He must have tossed it into the cupboard the last time he showered. His mother glared at it. "Just look at this dirty old towel, all crumpled up in a ball! Disgusting, Josh." She gave it a kick with the toe of her shoe. "Put it in the washbasket—now! I want this mess tidied up."

"Yes, Mum."

His mother's eyes strayed to the computer monitor on his desk. "Games, games, games, that's your trouble. You'd better not be playing games and ignoring your homework."

"No, Mum."

The homework. Oh no, he'd forgotten that too.

"Get your life straightened out, Josh," his mother said, leaving the room. "I'm not telling you again. No more games."

Mrs Matheson, Josh's teacher, went around the class collecting her students' homework.

Josh wondered if he should hand in an empty exercise book. It might buy him some time. He could always say it was a mistake, and that he'd handed in the wrong book.

No. Mrs Matheson, a stiff, beaky woman with curly grey hair that looked like a judge's wig, would just as likely open his exercise book then and there to check on him. It could make things worse for him, if that were possible.

She stopped at his desk. "And where's your essay, Josh Wilson?"

"I haven't finished it."

"Now that doesn't surprise me. Suppose you show me the start you've made."

"I can't. I haven't written it down yet. It's all in my head."

"You haven't started it yet."

"I haven't started it yet. But I've been thinking a lot about ancient Egypt," he said truthfully. "When it's finished it will be pretty good."

"Well, I'm finished with you. My patience is at an end. I am going to speak to the principal right now and have her call your mother. Go to the front of the room and keep an eye on the class while I'm out."

"Yes, Mrs Matheson."

Colouring to his ear tips, Josh dragged himself out of his chair and went to the teacher's desk. Putting him in charge was a subtle form of punishment in itself. If the class mucked up while she was away and he didn't report anybody, he'd be in worse trouble with Mrs Matheson. But if he did report anybody, he'd be in trouble with the class.

The principal's office was just down the hall. Mrs Matheson would hear if anyone misbehaved.

He stood near her desk, trying to avoid the smirks of the class. Paper aeroplanes and rolled-up paper missiles started to fly. Some boys ran after them.

"Sit down," Josh pleaded with them.

Just as two boys at the back started a ruler fight to see who could smash the other's ruler first, Mrs Matheson came back. "Go to your desk," she said to Josh coldly. She turned to the class. "Tomorrow we have our excursion to the Egyptian room at the museum," she announced. "Don't forget."

No one was listening. The whole class was too busy trying not to laugh. The chuckle began as a ripple, a little wave tripping over a stone. But it quickly gained force, washing through the room in a gurgle of merriment.

"What is so funny?" Mrs Matheson said sharply.

The laughter became a roar.

Everyone was staring at the teacher's desk. A girl at the front pointed. Mrs Matheson looked down.

Josh groaned.

A single human eye the size of a boiled egg was sitting on the desk. It looked like an artificial eye, but Josh knew differently. It was the eye of Osiris.

"I told you to keep an eye on the class and this is your idea of a joke. Take that disgusting thing off my desk, Josh. Throw it in my wastebasket."

Josh reached out for it reluctantly. It changed before he could touch it. When he picked it up, he saw that it was made of plastic, a joke eye from a novelty shop. The white was rivered with red veins. One of the boys must have put it there to get him into trouble.

But I know what I saw, he thought. It hadn't been a joke eye before. Or had it?

He dropped the eye into the wastebasket.

"For that prank, your essay will now be twenty pages long," Mrs Matheson told him.

Twenty pages!

When Josh and Amy arrived home from school, Harry was waiting for them. He looked bright-eyed and excited.

"You've been playing without us again," Josh said.

"Sorry," Harry said. "I was trying to save us a bit of time. More things have been coming through, you see. Scary things. I was taking a long hot shower this morning and the bathroom was full of steam. I reached out for a white towel on the rack, but guess what? I thought it was a towel, but it wasn't. It was the white kilt of that creepy guy with the snake's head. I'll swear it. I saw him standing sideways in the mist, staring at me with his shiny little eye. I yelled and Tina came running upstairs, barking. He vanished. But it got me moving, I can tell you! I decided to get back to the game. We've only got the body and heart of Osiris to go. I won back the eye!"

Josh was amazed. What did it take to scare his cousin? Harry still thought the game was safe, even after what had happened. Didn't he understand that it could harm him?

Oh well, at least he had regained the eye. That must have triggered the haunting, Josh guessed. But why was the game haunting them? To frighten them? He told Harry what had happened.

"Sorry, Josh." Harry couldn't help grinning. "But that's pretty funny if you think about it. Keeping an eye on the class! The Mummy Monster Game has a sense of humour."

"Yeah?" Josh said. "Well, maybe I don't."

"I don't think the game's funny at all," Amy said. "It's stolen Spy. When am I going to get him back? The poor thing must be terrified in there."

"You carry on at the controls," Josh said to Harry. "You won back the eye."

Harry moved the tiny figures on the screen along a passage. Their next challenge was to find the body of Osiris.

A box appeared on the screen:

YOU ARE ENTERING A PYRAMID THAT IS A MAZE OF PASSAGES. THE BODY OF OSIRIS IS AT THE END OF ONE OF THESE PASSAGES, BUT THERE ARE OBSTACLES ALONG THE WAY, DEAD ENDS, PASSWORDS

YOU HAVE TO KNOW AND, MOST DANGEROUS
OF ALL—PHARAOH PHANTOMS. IF THESE GHOSTS
CATCH YOU, YOUR CHARACTERS WILL DISAPPEAR.
THE ONLY WAY YOU CAN STOP THEM IS TO SHINE
YOUR TORCHES ON THEM. THEY ARE DESTROYED
BY LIGHT. BUT BE WARNED: THEY CAN APPEAR
SUDDENLY AROUND A CORNER, OR FLOAT OUT OF
A PASSAGE. ONE TOUCH FROM THEIR BANDAGED
FINGERS AND YOUR CHARACTERS WILL DISAPPEAR.
YOUR LIGHT IS YOUR WEAPON.

"Great!" Harry said. "A shoot-'em-up game! Our
torches become laser guns. We'll just leave them on and
flash them around everywhere."

THERE IS ONE MORE THING YOU NEED TO KNOW.
THE POWER IN YOUR TORCHES IS DRAINING.
YOU HAVE NO MORE THAN A FEW MINUTES LEFT
IN THEM. YOU HAD BETTER SWITCH THEM OFF
AND SAVE THEM OR YOU WILL BE LEFT WITHOUT
WEAPONS. THIS WILL PLACE YOU AT THE MERCY
OF THE PHARAOH PHANTOMS.

"Not so great," Harry said.

A dim light in the passages shone from some unseen
source above, bright enough to show the way ahead, but
not bright enough to harm the pharaoh phantoms.
Harry flicked the "fire" button on the joystick, and
lights moved ahead of the characters as if they were
carrying torches. He took his finger off the button to
save power.

The group of figures on the screen closed up

nervously and started along a passage.

"Watch out for pharaoh phantoms," Harry said. "I'll look ahead. Josh, you keep an eye on the side passages. Amy, keep watch behind us." Harry was enjoying himself. His voice was an excited whisper.

Passages started to open up all around them. There was no way of knowing which was the right one. They would just have to proceed by trial and error.

"I'll follow my nose," Harry said, turning off at a new passage.

A figure stepped in front of the group.

Three torch beams blasted it as Harry pressed the "fire" button.

It wasn't a pharaoh phantom.

13

Pharaoh Phantoms

The challenger was a muscular Nubian soldier with a shiny black torso. He was armed with a sword. As he appeared, a box also jumped on to the screen:

> TO ENTER THIS PASSAGE, YOU MUST GIVE THE PASSWORD TO THE GUARDIAN. NAME ONE OF THE SONS OF HORUS WHO GUARDS THE CANOPIC JARS.

Harry took his finger off the "fire" button. "I'll give you all four names," he said, typing them in. "Hapi the baboon-headed, Amset the human-headed, Duamutef the dog-headed, Qebehsenuf the falcon-headed."

The guardian bowed and stepped aside.

"Very clever, Harry," Amy said. "How did you remember all those?"

"Not too hard," Harry replied. "Mum's got a set of canopic jars at home in her study."

They followed the passage. It zigzagged, and was intersected by other passages.

Amy screamed.

Harry spun the characters around.

A pharaoh phantom, a glowing mummy figure with

its tattered finger outstretched, came floating along the passage behind them.

"Fire!" Harry shouted, stabbing the "fire" button on the joystick. The torch beams snapped on the phantom like lasers, and it disintegrated in a flash of light. It threw up its arms and gave a realistic cry, dry and dusty like a frog's croak.

Amy cheered.

"I think he just croaked," Harry said.

"Good shooting, Harry."

"Not bad," Josh said.

"Thanks," Harry said. The tiny explorers continued through the maze. When they came to a dead end, Harry turned them around and went back. He chose another passage.

A second Nubian guard stepped out in front of them. Harry kept his finger off the "fire" button this time. Another box appeared.

TO ENTER THIS PASSAGE, YOU MUST GIVE THE PASSWORD TO THE GUARDIAN. NAME ANOTHER OF THE SONS OF HORUS WHO GUARDS THE CANOPIC JARS.

"My answer is already given," Harry said.

The Nubian raised his sword threateningly.

"What's wrong?" Harry said, puzzled. "Does he want me to give them all again?"

"I think you have to give the names one by one," Josh said. "You've given one. Quick, what's the second name?"

The Nubian soldier took a step closer. The blade glinted above his head.

"Hapi the baboon-headed," Harry said, typing in the second name he had given earlier. Up came a box:

YOU HAVE ALREADY GIVEN THAT NAME.

The sword quivered in the Nubian's hands. Harry quickly typed in another name. "Amset the human-headed."

The Nubian lowered his sword and bowed.

"The game must have a few bugs in it," Harry said.

"No, it takes answers in the order you give them," Josh said reprovingly. "That's what you get for showing off."

They met two other Nubian guards, and Harry gave the other two names.

Josh did not see the phantom drifting out of a passage, its finger extended to touch them.

"Pharaoh phantom to our left!" Amy shouted.

It was almost touching the figure of the girl on the screen. Harry spun the characters round and punched the "fire" button again.

C-r-o-a-k! The pharaoh phantom flashed and disappeared.

"We must keep our minds on the game," Harry said.

In the next passage there were different obstacles.

A shiny black scorpion came scuttling down the passage towards them, and immediately a box appeared on the screen.

YOU MUST AVOID THESE SCORPIONS, OR THEY WILL KILL YOUR CHARACTERS. TO JUMP OVER THEM, PULL BACK THE JOYSTICK.

The scorpion scurried up to them like a metallic crab,

its pincer claws held out, the poison barb of its deadly tail reared wickedly. Harry waited until it was almost on them, then stabbed the "fire" button as he dragged back on the stick. The characters jumped in the air, allowing the scorpion to scuttle underneath.

"Here comes another one, Harry!"

They leaped again.

Amy gave a yell and jumped in her chair. Harry almost dropped the controls.

"What's the matter, Amy?"

"Something ran over my foot under the desk!"

"It can't have."

"I felt something!" She drew up her legs so that just the toes of her shoes touched the floor.

"Keep your mind on the game," Josh warned them. "It's just trying to distract us."

The scorpions were coming every few seconds. Josh hoped a pharaoh phantom wouldn't appear at the same moment as a scorpion. It did. Just as a scorpion neared the group, a phantom stepped out of a passage in front of their characters. Harry had to choose. Should he shoot the phantom or make the characters jump clear of the scorpion?

Harry's character jumped, but while he was still coming down, Harry rattled the "fire" button. The phantom vanished in a flash of light.

"Croaked another one," Harry chortled.

"I want a turn," Josh said.

"Okay, I reckon I need a break." Harry handed over the controls. Josh was still taking hold of them when Amy cried a warning. A pharaoh phantom had floated into the passage like mist.

"Phantom to your right, Josh!"

Josh's thumb hit the "fire" button.

C-r-o-a-k! In a flash of light the phantom was destroyed.

That was frighteningly close! But there was no time to relax. Here came another shiny, metallic marcher with its barb stuck in the air. Josh remembered to wait until the scorpion had reached the characters' feet. If they jumped too soon, they might land on it, and risked being stung.

"Now!"

He hit the "fire" button and pulled back on the stick. The three figures on the screen bounded into the air. The scorpion scurried underneath. Josh was getting the feel of it.

Another scorpion. They jumped—a little too early. The girl at the back almost landed on a stinging tail.

A pharaoh phantom stepped out abruptly from a side passage. Josh fired. The torches in the characters' hands gave a feeble flicker. Oh no, they were running out of light, and all at the same time!

Josh rattled the "fire" button on the joystick. The torch beams on the screen flickered again, but did not come to life.

The pharaoh phantom gave a sigh of satisfaction and started to drift towards them, its hand extended.

Josh stabbed the "fire" button. The torches glimmered, then spurted yellow beams.

C-r-o-a-k!

The pharaoh phantom disappeared in a flash, and so

did their torch lights. Now they were in darkness.

Josh chose another passage. Something stepped out in front of them. A pharaoh phantom? He tried the "fire" button. Nothing.

"It's only a guardian," Harry said in a choked voice as if he hadn't taken a breath for a few minutes. He released the air with a loud sigh.

This guardian was a bald-headed Egyptian bowman. He had an arrow nocked to his bow and was pointing it at the group. Once more the familiar box appeared:

TO ENTER THIS PASSAGE, YOU MUST GIVE THE PASSWORD TO THE GUARDIAN. WHAT IS THE NAME OF A GREAT HOUSE AND A KING?

"Pharaoh," Josh said.

He typed it in. The bowman lowered his bow and withdrew into the shadows. Josh took the characters along the passage.

The game, warming up, emitted a hum that grew to a whine. The lines of perspective began to pulse again. Josh felt their hypnotic pull. The lines blasted to the centre of the screen, and Josh felt himself being tugged bodily forward. The lines swept him into the passage. He was flying, and the others were flying with him. The cold gullet of a stone passage swallowed them. They were travelling along it to meet a pinpoint of light. The pinpoint flashed.

They landed in the passage, running, their bodies jarring with the impact of their feet on the stone floor. Once again the game had become real around them. But the passage they were following ended abruptly.

"Oh no," Amy said.

The stone floor fell away into a black chasm.

"Look, there's a way over," Harry said. "There's a rope dangling into the pit."

"Yes, but we'll never reach it," Josh said. "It's too far."

"Jump."

"What if we miss?"

"We won't. You go first. Grab the end and swing on it until it takes you to the other side. Then swing the rope back to us."

"What if one of us is busy swinging when a pharaoh phantom comes?" Amy said anxiously.

"Don't think about it," Harry said.

Josh, Amy and Harry went nervously to the edge of the pit. The length of motionless rope, disappearing into the void, seemed impossibly far away. Josh swallowed.

"Good luck, Josh."

Something was happening. The passages that converged on theirs were filled with glowing white shapes like puffs of mist. Pharaoh phantoms. They were approaching from every direction.

Josh moved right up to the edge of the chasm.

"Do something, Josh!" Amy said, grabbing his arm. The movement made him teeter dangerously on the brink.

"Watch it, Amy!"

"Sorry. But this is so scary!"

Josh bent his knees. The muscles in his legs felt shivery, as if they might seize up and refuse to launch him. The rope seemed to move even further away.

Josh jumped into the void. He sailed through space, hit the rope, clung to it and hung over the pit, the arc of his swing slowly widening. How close were the pharaoh phantoms now? The arc of the swing now brought him to the other side of the chasm. He landed and twisted around, still holding the rope. Then he gave the rope a hard push. It swung back across the pit.

Harry caught it, and sailed towards Josh in a long pendulum swing.

Pharaoh phantoms floated out of the surrounding passages. Amy screamed. The sight of them broke Harry's concentration. He forgot to let go of the rope and he swung back towards Amy, his weight making the rope move swiftly. The pharaoh phantoms were all around Amy now, their fingers extending to touch her.

Was there room on the rope for Amy too? Harry swung over to the far side again. Amy shrank towards the edge of the pit. The phantoms had gathered in a ring around her.

Now Harry was swinging back. He started to slide down the rope, making room for Amy to hold on too. "Jump, Amy!" he called to her.

Amy sprang like a cricket, caught the rope, and grabbed it tightly. Now the two of them were swinging across the void. On the other side, Josh tried to catch the rope, but missed.

"Josh, are you here?"

It was their mother calling! Her voice spiralled towards them as if it was travelling down the length of the tunnel. She had come into the bedroom!

Josh twisted around, horrified.

"What's going on, Josh?" their mother shouted. "It's pitch black in here!"

Startled, Harry and Amy missed their chance of jumping off the rope on Josh's side. They swung back across the chasm to where the phantoms waited for them, their bandaged hands outstretched.

Josh's thoughts raced. *What's Mum doing home this early? Why didn't she toot the horn? Never mind that now. What about Amy and Harry?*

"Good," he heard his mother say. "Caught you at it! I see a game on the computer. I've just been to your school to see your principal. Josh, I'm sick of you neglecting your homework to play mindless computer games. I did warn you. Now I'm going to teach you a lesson and confiscate your computer for one week. So you'd better come out, wherever you are."

Swinging on the rope, Amy and Harry touched the edge of the chasm. The pharaoh phantoms lunged forward. There were two flashes of light, and the two children dropped away. Just like that. The rope swung slackly across the void.

Amy and Harry were gone. The phantoms disappeared too, blown away like leaves in a gust of wind.

Josh looked in horror at the empty, swinging rope. Beyond it he could see the passage running all the way to his bedroom. He saw his mother far away, as if through a shrinking lens. She moved towards the computer.

Josh found his voice. "Mum, don't turn it off! Not now!"

14

Grounded

Josh grabbed the dangling rope and swung back to the other side. He saw the glowing lines stretching along the passage back to his room.

"Mum, let me finish the game, please."

He must stop her! He ran.

The bedroom opened up around him in a flash, and he grabbed his mother's arm as she bent towards the switch.

"Let go of me, Josh!" his mother said, irritably.

"Mum, please!"

There were three empty chairs in front of the monitor.

Josh stared at the screen. Amy and Harry's characters had vanished. *Quick, what can I do? Maybe if I can finish the challenge, reach the sanctuary at the end of the passage, I can save them.*

He broke away from his mother and dived back to the computer controls.

In her determination to switch off the computer, his mother now made a grab for the cord. She groped for it, but couldn't find it in the dark.

Josh sped the last surviving character back down the passage and made him leap on to the rope. He swung him back across the chasm to the other side and raced him along the passage.

The passage opened into a chamber, and there lay the body of Osiris on a stone altar. Apart from this the chamber was empty. The walls were covered with carved reliefs showing a dead king's journey by boat along the underworld Nile. There was no guardian, Josh noticed thankfully. He dreaded another challenge. It had been enough of a challenge to cross the chasm!

What did he have to do to win the body of Osiris? Touch it?

He didn't have to. When his character on the screen reached the altar, the mummified trunk of Osiris exploded in strands of light, as though the bandages were flying out like streamers. Then, abruptly, it vanished. The slab was bare. Where had the body gone? *No time to worry about that now,* Josh told himself.

He had reached the goal, and won the body of Osiris!

And his mother had reached the plug. She tugged it out of its socket.

The screen of the computer went black, except for a shrinking square of light that disappeared into nothingness.

"Mum, what have you done?" Josh said in a strangled voice.

"I've put an end to the game."

"You've put an end to our lives!"

"There's more to life than computer games, Josh. It's time you learnt that. Now pack up the computer and put it downstairs in my study. I forbid you to play another computer game in this house until I see some change in you. You can begin by completing that essay you were supposed to write for your homework. Where have Amy and Harry got to? You'll have to make your own supper tonight. I have to go back to the office now and I'll be working late, very late. Where are they?"

"Who?" he asked numbly.

"Amy and Harry."

"I don't know. They've disappeared somewhere," he heard himself say.

He couldn't tell his mother what had happened. He couldn't begin to tell her. He didn't know himself.

Under his mother's instructions, he packed up the computer and put it downstairs in her study, but he didn't plug it in and switch it on. He left the screen dead, the way he was feeling inside.

The weather changed after his mother left the house.

Thunder dragged its grumbling belly over the suburbs. Lightning flashed across the sky. It began to rain.

Where were Amy and Harry—and Spy? Maybe they had materialised in a cupboard, like the foot of Osiris. He made a check of the house, beginning with his own wardrobe, and then opening every cupboard, looking under every bed.

"Amy! Harry! If you're here, please come out."

The empty house sneered at him.

They were gone, but where? Josh remembered how the image of the game on the screen had shrunk to a spot of light after his mother had pulled out the plug. Had Amy and Harry been sucked into the electronic unconsciousness of the computer? Or had they simply

114

de-materialised?

What could he do?

Josh felt like hiding in a cupboard himself. He went into Amy's bedroom. It was a neat room with a pretty floral cover on the bed. A white bear with a stitched-on smile sat on the mantelpiece. Josh had won it for Amy at the Show. She'd been so proud of him.

She wouldn't be proud of him now. He'd failed, and he was miserably afraid.

"Amy, I don't know what to do."

He picked up the white bear and sat on his sister's bed, holding it. The bear's glassy eyes, rather too closely set, squinted at him expectantly.

I can't take any more of this, Josh thought. It's too scary for me. What do I do? Who do I go to for help? The police? My school? My mother?

No one would believe him.

Then he recalled the game's warning. Worse things might start coming through.

There was only one answer—to run away.

I wish I was the big brother Amy deserved. He pictured Amy's clear grey eyes gazing at him knowingly. *I wish I was someone big and brave that Harry could look up to.* In his imagination he saw Harry's bright eyes, expecting so much of him. *But I'm just a pretender who's been putting on an act.*

If he truly were the brother he should be, and if he truly were the older cousin Harry could look up to, he would try to find a way out of this mess.

The bear's stitched-on smile caught his eye. He imagined Amy smiling.

Pretender. But maybe that was all you could ever be in the face of fear. Nobody in the world was really brave. Everybody felt fear. Bravery was merely pretending you could overlook the fear. So instead of pretending less, maybe Josh should pretend a little more. Pretend to be fearless. Like Harry.

What would fearless Harry do?

He'd go back and finish the game. *The difference is, I'm not Harry. I'm Josh. I don't think the world is safe and I don't think the game is safe. The game is heartless. It will destroy me too. But I must play on.*

Alone? Without the comforting presence of Amy and Harry?

Yes.

Risking the danger of disappearing as Amy and Harry had done?

Yes.

Against his mother's wishes?

Yes, again.

He'd have to go back on the computer and try to finish the quest.

It may not be over, a thought whispered to him. He had made it across the pit and had reached the body of Osiris. The game had a memory—maybe he could pick up where he'd left off. If he could complete the quest, then perhaps he had some chance of putting things right, of bringing Amy and Harry back.

He looked at the window. A flurry of raindrops blew against it. The drops slid in cold tears down the window-pane. Josh imagined Amy alone somewhere, crying for help, like the figure of Isis in the game.

After a while the rain stopped.

Josh put the bear back on Amy's mantelpiece.

"I'm going to play on," he said out loud. "Hang on, Amy, Harry, Spy … I'm going to try to win you back—even if I get swallowed up trying!"

Josh went down to his mother's study. It was furnished like an office, with a filing cabinet and an office desk and a fax machine in a corner. He plugged in the computer and turned it on, then switched on a green-shaded banker's lamp on the desk. It threw a hazy greenish light.

Pretend you're not afraid, Josh told himself. *Keep pretending.*

He sat at the desk and loaded up the game. His heart was thudding against his ribs, and he swallowed hard as the game came to life on the screen. The familiar creepy Egyptian music floated out of the monitor and filled the study. He wished Amy and Harry were with him. Josh glanced nervously around his mother's efficiently organised study. There wasn't a piece of paper out of place.

Efficiency. Think efficiency. Play with efficiency. No mistakes. He had to beat this game to get Harry and Amy back, but he couldn't do it unless he stayed cool.

As he'd hoped, the game picked up where he'd left off. The solitary adventurer on the screen followed a stone passage lit by flickering wall lamps.

A box with writing on it blocked out the picture. Josh had to keep scrolling to read it all.

YOU MUST NOW FIND THE MOST PRECIOUS FRAG-

MENT OF ALL, THE HEART OF OSIRIS, SYMBOLISED BY THE PROTECTIVE HEART-SCARAB. THE ANCIENT EGYPTIANS BELIEVED THAT THE HEART WAS THE SEAT OF THE SOUL. THAT WAS WHY, WHEN A MAN DIED AND WENT BEFORE THE JUDGES IN THE HALL OF JUDGEMENT, A SYMBOL OF HIS HEART WAS WEIGHED IN A SET OF SCALES TO DETERMINE WHETHER HE HAD LIVED A GOOD LIFE OR AN EVIL ONE. HIS HEART WAS PLACED IN ONE PAN OF THE SCALES AND A SINGLE FEATHER, REPRESENTING TRUTH, WAS PLACED IN THE OTHER. IF HIS HEART WAS LIGHT—INNOCENT OF EVIL-DOING—IT WOULD NOT TIP THE SCALES. IF HE WERE EVIL AND HIS HEART WAS HEAVY ENOUGH TO TIP THE SCALES, THEN HIS SOUL WOULD BE DEVOURED BY A MONSTER WAITING IN THE PIT OF EVERLASTING NOTHINGNESS. THIS MONSTER, THE "DEVOURER OF SOULS", IS KNOWN AS AMMIT. SHE HAS THE HEAD OF A CROCODILE, THE TRUNK AND FORE-PAWS OF A LION, AND THE HINDQUARTERS OF A HIPPOPOTAMUS. THIS MONSTER GUARDS THE HEART OF OSIRIS. TO DEFEAT HER, YOU MUST DEFEAT EACH SEPARATE PART OF HER BODY. AND TO MAKE YOUR CHALLENGE HARDER, THE THREE PARTS OF AMMIT WILL NOT BE SEEN TOGETHER. FOR YOUR COMBAT YOU WILL BE GIVEN THREE MAGICAL WEAPONS: A BOW AND ARROW, A SPEAR AND A NOOSE OF ROPE THAT IS THE SACRED KNOT OF ISIS. TO DEFEAT THE DEVOURER OF SOULS, YOU MUST USE THEM IN THE RIGHT WAY. HERE IS YOUR CLUE:

I AM AMMIT, DEVOURER OF SOULS,
CREATURE FROM THE PIT.
TO DEFEAT ME YOU MUST KNOW
JUST WHERE YOUR BLOW MUST HIT.
A CROCODILE IS MY FRONT,
A LION IS MY MIDDLE,
A HIPPO MY HINDQUARTERS.
LISTEN TO MY RIDDLE.

MUCH DEPENDS ON WHERE YOU START:
THERE IS A SPECIAL WAY.
TAKE NOTE OF WHERE YOU MUST BEGIN.
TAKE NOTE OF WHAT I SAY.
FIRST MY REAR, THEN MY HEAD,
THEN FINALLY MY HEART.
STRIKE ME ON A DAPPLED STAIN AND I'LL
BLOW MYSELF APART.

Josh imagined Amy and Harry sitting beside him. *Pay attention to every detail*, he heard them warn him. He read the riddle again and fixed it in his mind. Then he read it out aloud, just to be sure.

He moved his character along a passage. The game wasn't drawing him in. Why? Would he be able to rescue Amy and Harry like this?

The scenery changed. Josh's character left the passage and came out into a swampy region among tall papyrus reeds at the edge of the River Nile. Light winked realistically on ripples on the water, and the reeds stirred in a breeze. Further out in the middle of the river, a smooth grey rock rose like a barren island. A blue glazed object shone on the island. It looked like an insect.

It must be the scarab beetle, Josh decided. He'd have to cross the water to get to it. But how was he supposed to reach the island? Swim? Not with that monster around. It could bite him in half.

Then he saw a skiff, a small boat made of papyrus reeds tied together, the flared ends swept up like an archer's bow. The boat was almost concealed by the reeds growing at the edge of the river.

Josh moved the solitary explorer on the screen towards the boat. I don't like the way the reeds are stirring, he thought. I hope that creature isn't hiding in there, waiting to pounce on me.

Josh moved his character on to the flat surface of the skiff. The weapons lay on the deck: the bow and arrow, the spear, and the rope with a noose at one end.

Unseen hands launched the boat from the bank: Realistic ripples spread around its bow and fanned out in its wake as it drifted across the sparkling green river towards the rock. Josh scanned the water, expecting the head of a crocodile to break the surface at any moment. Maybe this was going to be easier than he thought.

Bump. The prow of the skiff hit the side of the island. He had reached it safely. The jewelled scarab beetle now magically appeared on the deck of the boat.

Josh felt uneasy. He had won the heart, the final prize, but could it really be this simple? No, he still had to get it past the monster in three parts, he reminded himself. He had to run the gauntlet of the hippopotamus, the crocodile and the lion, and he had to destroy each one. This would be the real challenge.

"Let's get out of here," he said aloud. "There's something I don't like about that island."

Suddenly the rocky outcrop was no longer an island. It rose from the surface with a hiss of streaming water, the smooth back and rear legs of a monster hippopotamus.

15

A Monster in Three Parts

The hippopotamus looked bigger than a surfacing submarine. It was going to upset the boat!

A tidal wave of green water hit the tiny craft and flung it in the air like a leaf.

Use your weapons, quickly!

The hippopotamus was turning to chase him.

Josh used the cursor to pick up the bow and arrow. He squeezed the "fire" button on the joystick.

Wrong weapon. The bow wouldn't shoot.

Perhaps Egyptians used to hunt the hippopotamus with spears, Josh thought. He selected the spear and launched it at the creature's hindquarters.

There was a loud *crack* and a bomb-burst of flashing light. The hippopotamus vanished. Ripples spread out in concentric circles from where it had been.

Josh moved the skiff towards the bank. Where was the crocodile head? There was no sign of it. Now the scenery had changed. Instead of a reed-fringed river bank, he faced a vast overhanging cavern. What might be lurking in there?

He'd rather land his character somewhere else. He flicked the joystick to one side, trying to alter the course of the papyrus skiff, but it did not respond to the controls. It was making straight for the cave.

It must be a limestone cave, Josh thought. Stalactites hung like white icicles from the roof of the cave and stalagmites speared up from the floor, giving the impression of teeth in a huge mouth. The stone exterior of the cave had a greenish tinge. Perhaps it was covered with moss.

It was as if the whole cave were the open jaws of—

Josh gasped and went rigid. The skiff was floating straight into the jaws of a crocodile!

He looked at the weapons on the deck of the boat. Should he try the bow and arrow again? Or the rope? "How's a rope going to stop a monster crocodile?" he said aloud.

Then he remembered that this wasn't just any rope. It was the sacred knot of Isis. Maybe he could use it like a lasso.

He selected the rope from the deck and pressed "fire".

The rope uncoiled, flew into a loop around the jaws of the crocodile, then pulled itself tight, snapping the mouth shut. The jaws bit off the front of the skiff, but the crocodile was destroyed.

Crack! It disappeared in another bomb-burst flash.

Only the lion remained.

The character on the screen pocketed the scarab jewel, disembarked and proceeded on foot, away from the river.

Two creatures down, Josh thought, *and I still have the heart scarab of Osiris.*

Soon his character had walked into a desert valley flanked by two soaring cliffs. Was the lion at the end of this valley? The cliffs began to converge, the distance between them narrowing as he went further. Josh noticed something peculiar about their texture. They were covered with short, golden-brown scrub that looked almost like fur—the skin of a close-haired dog or a lion.

There's something weird about these cliffs, Josh thought, stopping the character on the screen. Were they cliffs—or paws? Was he going between the paws of a lion? If it was a lion, it must be bigger than the great sphinx.

The cliffs rumbled and began to move. Josh jumped in his seat. Giant claws closed around the little explorer on the screen. A roar came out of the monitor.

There was only one weapon left. Was the puny bow and arrow enough to stop a lion as big as a sphinx? Josh remembered what he had learnt about the way Egyptian pharaohs hunted lions in chariots. *Pharaohs journeyed into the desert to hunt lions from their chariots, using bows and arrows.*

He slid the cursor over the bow and arrow, then moved it to the lion's chest where the two great legs met. The chest was like the sheer side of a mountain, rising to a head that was in the clouds. He looked for his target, the dappled area half way up the mountainside. He remembered the clue: *Strike me on a dappled stain and I'll blow myself apart.* Positioning the cursor, he pressed the "fire" button. A little arrow sped from the bow with a whizzing sound. The cliffs erupted when it hit, breaking up and sending down an avalanche of stones.

Josh made his character jump into the air to clear the racing boulders under his feet.

The rest of the cliffs now disappeared in a flash of light. The heart-scarab rose out of his character's pocket and floated, shining, off the screen.

"I've done it! I've beaten you!" Josh shouted to the game.

The graphics vanished, the screen went blank, and Josh heard the original Egyptian theme music. A box appeared:

CONGRATULATIONS. YOU HAVE SUCCESSFULLY COMPLETED YOUR QUEST. YOU HAVE NOW ASSEMBLED ALL THE FRAGMENTS OF OSIRIS SO THAT HE MAY UNDERGO THE MYSTERY OF RESURRECTION AND TAKE HIS PLACE IN THE EGYPTIAN UNDERWORLD AS THE JUDGE OF THE DEAD. EVEN NOW THE PROCESS IS OCCURRING ...

The box disappeared and the scene changed. It went back to the first chamber, where Isis had wailed over the loss of Osiris. Now the view was from above the stone sarcophagus, looking down into it. Isis was at the edge, still weeping, but this time with joy. Something was happening. Fragments of a mummy were appearing in the sarcophagus. First a mummy's bandaged feet, then its legs, arms, head, insides, body, eye and scarab-heart. The pieces were moving, coming together. There was a dry, rustling sound. Light exploded around them and the pieces fused together.

Osiris was now complete, his mummy stretched out in the sarcophagus.

Isis gave a cry of joy.

Osiris rose from the stone sarcophagus and Isis held up her arms to show her delight and adoration.

"Great, you're together again. Now can I please have Harry and Amy back!" Josh said to the screen.

The screen flickered. A sound like static came from the monitor.

Another box appeared.

DISK ERROR. DISK ERROR. PROGRAMME DISK HAS BEEN VIOLATED.

The disk drive whirred frantically. Snatches of scenes from all the challenges flickered across the screen, accompanied by a swirling mixture of sound effects. Then the disk drive was silent, and an image filled the screen.

It was an Egyptian creature, standing sideways, surrounded by bright light. The creature had a man's body but the shadow-head of an animal Josh had never seen before. It had a drooping snout like an ant-eater, and strange, square-tipped, erect ears. Its single eye in profile beamed out a chill light that Josh could feel. He shivered.

A box appeared.

THIS IS SETH, THE EGYPTIAN DEVIL, THE EVIL BROTHER OF OSIRIS. HE IS ANGRY THAT YOU HAVE SOLVED THE CHALLENGES OF THE MUMMY MONSTER GAME AND HE NOW REFUSES TO RELEASE YOUR LOST ONES. IN A FINAL ACT OF

SPITE, SETH HAS TAMPERED WITH THE GAME SO THAT THEY MAY NOT BE REACHED. THE LOST ONES MUST SPEND ETERNITY LOCKED IN A DUNGEON IN THE PIT OF EVERLASTING NOTHINGNESS, GUARDED BY THE CROCODILE-HEADED ONE.

Seth disappeared, and a blinding light streamed from the computer screen.

Josh dropped the joystick. "This isn't supposed to happen," he shouted.

What could he do now? He felt a surge of anger. He had been cheated, tricked by the game. He had completed the quest only to discover a disastrous hitch. Where were Amy and Harry?

The screen flashed, the interruption was over, and Osiris and Isis reappeared, embracing. Words appeared in a box beneath them:

OSIRIS HAS TRIUMPHED OVER DEATH IN ORDER TO BRING TO ALL EGYPTIANS THE PROMISE OF ETERNAL SURVIVAL. HE WILL NOW ASSUME HIS RIGHTFUL PLACE IN THE EGYPTIAN UNDERWORLD, WHERE HE WILL REIGN AS KING AND SIT IN JUDGEMENT ON THE SOULS OF MEN.

"Never mind Osiris and the souls of men!" Josh said hotly. "Where are Amy and Harry? I want them back! I've played my part. I put Osiris together again, and I deserve to have Amy and Harry back. Let them go!"

Another box appeared beneath Osiris and Isis:

YOU MUST GO AFTER THE LOST ONES TO RESCUE

THEM. BUT YOU CAN NO LONGER REACH THEM
THROUGH THE GAME. THERE IS ONLY ONE WAY
TO REACH THEM, AND THAT IS THROUGH THE
DOORWAY OF A HOUSE OF ETERNITY. YOU MUST
FIND ONE.

"Find a house of eternity? How am I supposed to do
that!" Josh asked, exasperated.

THIS IS YOUR LAST CHALLENGE—AND LAST HOPE.
YOU MUST SEARCH FOR A REAL HOUSE OF ETERNITY.

Osiris and Isis vanished. The faint sounds of Egyptian
music trembled in the air, then faded.

The screen went blank. The disk drive spat out the
Mummy Monster Game programme. The game was over.

No Amy, no Harry!

Josh fell into a black pit of despair. He'd completed
the quest. He'd even solved the last challenge on his
own. He felt like shoving the computer off the desk and
smashing it to pieces.

"You've tricked me!" he yelled. He switched off the
computer angrily.

The glow of the blank screen shrank to a tiny dot and
vanished. Josh stared at the dead screen. What could
you expect from a game? Fairness? It didn't care about
fairness.

He had the sensation that the walls of the room were
closing around him, and with this came a breathless,
suffocating feeling. Amy and Harry were gone. What
could he do? Where could he look?

"Cheat!" he said to the computer. He took the game

out of the disk drive, and left.

There was nothing to do, nowhere to look. Where was he going to find an ancient Egyptian tomb in a modern city?

Josh felt tired, drained. A weight pressed on his shoulders. Maybe he should lie down. It might calm him and help him to think. He flopped on the couch, and Tina jumped up, nestled beside him and licked his cheek. He gave her a hug, finding her warmth comforting.

Games had caused all this. His obsession with games had brought him to disaster.

He thought of Amy and Harry, and remembered with shame how he'd wanted to impress them with his playing skills, to prove that he was the best game player of all. He felt a pang of longing for them. People weren't just objects to play against, things to beat. Amy and Harry counted for more. He didn't care if he never played another computer game in his life. He wanted his sister and his cousin back. Their disappearance had opened up a bottomless pit in his life. *A pit of everlasting nothingness*.

He had never felt so empty in his life.

Finally Josh drifted into exhausted sleep. His dreams were filled with pharaoh phantoms. They came floating out of tunnels towards the couch where he lay, their outstretched fingers pointing accusingly at him. Then he pictured Amy and Harry swinging over the chasm. He saw his mother pulling the cord from the wall. He saw Amy and Harry tumbling down, down into the darkness, into a pit of everlasting nothingness.

Waiting for them at the bottom of the pit was the crocodile-headed mummy monster, licking its scaly jaws.

The shadows in the room were growing darker when Josh's eyes sprang open. What time was it? His mother hadn't come home yet.

He sat up so suddenly that Tina gave a yelp of surprise.

I can't just sit here, Josh thought. *There must be something I can do. Think, think.*

For every problem there is a solution. That was the rule of computer games. But was it the rule of life? Games were predictable: they had distinct boundaries, laws and rewards. In life things were different. Rules were applied inconsistently, whether they were rules at school or rules at home. Josh's mother set only the vaguest boundaries, and she ignored his repeated crossing of them. For a time. Then, unpredictably, she'd go off pop. It was the same at school. Sometimes you were punished for breaking the rules and sometimes you weren't. Sometimes you were rewarded for doing well and sometimes you weren't.

Mentally Josh went over every detail of the game. He felt his mind humming like a disk drive as it frantically sought a solution. Then the answer popped out of his brain with a clear *ping*, like the sound his computer made when it discharged a disk from the drive.

"I know where I'll find a house of eternity," Josh said aloud. He remembered now. It was something he had learnt earlier in the game. A house of eternity meant two things: a tomb, and a coffin—a coffin decorated with magical texts from the Egyptian Book of the Dead and fitted with false doors for the soul. Josh had seen them—real ones—in the museum.

That was his answer. He would find a house of eternity in the Egyptian room of the museum in the city. Maybe he could open and enter one of those doorways to eternity and set Harry and Amy free.

The museum was his last hope. He'd better go there and look. He glanced at his watch, and groaned with frustration. Too late. The museum would be closed.

Don't panic yet. There's still a chance. Go in the morning.

But what would he tell his mother tonight? Maybe she'd be really late, so late that she wouldn't bother to check on them in their beds. Unlikely. She always checked on them. He'd better take precautions and stuff pillows under Harry's and Amy's blankets so they looked as if they were safely asleep.

He needed time.

16

The Museum Visit

"Where is your sister? And where is Harry?"

Josh's mother came into the kitchen with Tina prancing at her feet. She cast a glance around the kitchen. There were no plates or empty cups in evidence.

"Er, they got up early. Harry walked with Amy to school," Josh said.

"She didn't eat any breakfast."

"She wasn't hungry. She disappeared in a hurry."

"Don't *you* be late. It's funny that Amy didn't say goodbye." She opened a can of dog food for Tina, and put the bowl on the floor. "Seen the cat?" she asked Josh.

"Spy?" He shrugged. "No. You know how Spy just vanishes."

His mother made herself some coffee and went back to her bedroom to dress for work.

Josh sucked in a big lungful of air as he rolled towards the city. The skateboard's wheels ran smoothly over the pavement, sending only the faintest soothing vibrations through the soles of his sneakers and up through his legs.

The cheerful, sunny morning gave him hope.

He scooted past the spot where he had overtaken the new boy on the skateboard. He felt a twinge of guilt, but quickly shrugged it aside.

Crossing the road, he turned towards the city.

Josh went up the stairs to the second level of the museum, carrying his skateboard under his arm.

The Egyptian room, its walls decorated with bright frescoes, was deserted. It was like going into a tomb. Josh saw the rippled coils of an underworld serpent; painted gods, goddesses and pharaohs. A ceiling fan threw shadows that made the images stir. Flat wooden cases with glass tops occupied the middle of the room. Josh saw an orange-coloured mummy in a case directly ahead of him, and beneath that a detached mummy's head that was blackened like a chunk of coal. Near it was a pair of fine-boned mummified feet with painted toenails.

A black statue of a pharaoh with clenched fists sat on a throne near the doorway. Josh walked around it, his shoes squeaking in the enclosed space of the room. He came to some glass cases crammed with amulets and small figurines of Egyptian gods in the form of cats, ibis, baboons and jackals. Among them was a small statue of Isis and also one of Osiris in the form of a mummy, clasping the crook and flail of kingship. He scowled at it. *It's okay for you, Osiris, you're safely back in one piece*, he thought. *But what about Amy and Harry?* He moved on. His attention was taken by the mummy of a woman stretched out in a glass case. She lay tightly wrapped in the sleep of eternity, resting on the base of her wooden coffin. The decorated lid of the coffin had been raised on supports above her so that visitors could look inside.

A sign identified the exhibit as the 2000-year-old mummified body of an Egyptian lady.

Josh looked around for the coffins. He discovered a row of them standing upright in a tall glass display case at the back of the room: wooden coffins, human in shape, with heads and painted faces.

The eyes on the coffins seemed to seek him out. Would one of these houses of eternity contain a doorway that would lead him to Amy and Harry? Which one? That bulky wooden coffin with big carved ears and eyes that were as round and mysterious as black planets? Or one of the others?

An arched doorway led to another room. There must be a second Egyptian room now. Josh remembered only one. He went through the doorway.

It was as if he were playing the Mummy Monster Game again.

Far off, like an echo, Josh heard the wailing of Isis, and again a trickle of fear slid down his back. *He was in the original burial chamber, the one they had first seen in the game.*

It was the same rectangular room. Scenes from the Book of the Dead and the underworld journey of the soul crowded every centimetre of the walls, which were covered with a starry horde of gods, goddesses and creatures on a night sky. And there, spanning the entire ceiling, was the outstretched figure of the sky goddess Nut.

How was it possible?

How did the game know that this room existed?

Josh gazed at the stone sarcophagus. Was this the sarcophagus where the fragments of Osiris had come together? Was he still inside? Josh went closer and, nervously, peered over the edge. It was empty.

Calm down. Look around.

The burial chamber was exactly the same as the one in the game, except for one difference. It had another exit—or at least what looked like a shadowy doorway going through the wall. But was it a doorway? It was vaguely human shaped. Was it a coffin? It had no lid. Maybe it was the base of a coffin.

Josh went nearer. He put out his hand to touch the doorway, and his hand disappeared into the darkness. It *was* a doorway.

Josh wasn't scared for himself any more. All he could think of was Amy and Harry. This was his chance to help them, to make up for what he had done. Amy and Harry were somewhere beyond that doorway. They needed him.

With the skateboard under his arm, Josh stepped boldly over the threshold.

17

Passages and Pits

It was like breaking through a cobweb. The shadow gave the slightest resistance to his body, wrapping itself around him, clinging to his arms and face and hair, and then it snapped.

Goosebumps rose on Josh's skin. But he was through the shadow, and into the darkness of a passage that flung itself to infinity.

The museum had gone.

Josh glimpsed the texture of stone walls sliding past him. He was on a rise. The floor was smooth: he could go faster on his skateboard. He put the board down and set off, paddling with one leg, gaining speed. The enclosing walls accentuated the rumble of his wheels. Small oil lamps in alcoves set into the walls threw wobbly shadows around the passage.

I'm coming, Amy! I'm coming, Harry!

An armour-plated scorpion came scuttling to meet him, its barbed tail reared, its pincers spread to grapple. It was the size of a rat.

Josh steered the board to one side and curved out of its path. Another scorpion took its place, and another.

It was like doing a slalom between poles. Josh snaked his way along the passage.

Now a vast army of scorpions advanced. There was no way Josh could weave between them. If only he was on a downward slope! Then he could simply coast on his board, without placing a foot on the floor. He had an idea. Maybe he should ride beside the wall and pull himself along, using the wall for purchase.

He gave one final hard push with the toe of his sneaker and coasted towards the wall. His front wheels hit an advance pair of scorpions, which burst with a sound like jacaranda pods popping under the soles of shoes. A signal of panic ran through the scorpions, and they cleared a path for the skateboard. Josh was losing speed now. But if he put his foot down, even for an instant, a scorpion might run up his leg and lash at him with its poisonous tail.

The scorpions saw him slowing, and closed in. The skateboard limped towards the wall. Josh heard the drumming sound of dozens of scorpions striking with their tails at the underbelly of the board. His skin shivered.

He used the wall to drag himself, hand over hand, along the passageway. The scuttling and scraping of the sea of metallic bodies was like the hiss of surf running up a beach.

Josh worked his way further. The floor of the passage began to drop away, and the skateboard took speed from the slope. The scorpions parted to avoid the run of the hard, crushing wheels.

Josh sped through them. Then the passage turned, and they were gone.

Josh rolled on, propelling himself with the occasional thrust of his foot. Other tunnels opened into the main passage, but he flashed past them and pulled up at the edge of a chasm.

A single rope hung limply into the blackness. Josh gaped at the pit. It gaped back.

How am I supposed to cross with a skateboard? he wondered. Should I leave it on this side? What if I hit more scorpions on the other side? Maybe I should choose another route, take one of the tunnels that joins this one.

He left his board at the edge of the pit and went to examine the other tunnels. Gloomy. Scary. He could hear sounds inside them, shuffling, swishing sounds. Pharaoh phantoms!

Josh made a decision. He'd have to go without the board.

He measured the distance between himself and the dangling rope. He would need to lean forward to give himself the right angle. Not too far, or he'd fall.

The shuffling sounds drew nearer.

Would the rope hold him? It looked ancient and frayed. It was probably thousands of years old, rotten and hanging by a thread.

Too late now. Josh launched himself into space. His open fingers hit the rough *halfa*-grass fibre and clamped around it, but his weight pulled him into the chasm. He hooked a leg around the rope to steady himself, and stopped sliding. The rope held.

It's not going to break. It's going to hold me. Climb up.

Josh worked his way a bit higher, then began to

swing himself, extending the arc of his swing until he was alternately bumping each side of the chasm.

One more swing would do it.

He saw something in one of the tunnels, and twisted. Dim white shapes were emerging, blurs of movement—pharaoh phantoms!

Josh made a long pendulum swing.

He landed safely on the other side, careful to keep hold of the rope. The shuffling noise grew until it sounded like a steam train.

He jammed one end of the rope into a crack at the side of the chasm so that it would be ready for the swing back. White, bandaged shapes with extended arms shuffled out of the tunnels. Josh ran.

The level of the passage dropped swiftly to meet a flight of dimly lit stone steps that corkscrewed downwards. Josh followed the steps down and down until he reached the floor. At the end of a corridor he came to the barred wall of a dungeon. Sleeping on a stone slab in front of it was the guardian of the dungeon—the mummy monster.

18

Prisoners of the Mummy Monster

Amy and Harry were behind bars, sitting on piles of straw. Amy was holding a ginger cat in her arms, stroking its ears absently. She'd found Spy! Harry sat glumly, his head in his hands.

Josh wanted to cry out to them: "Amy! Harry! I'm here!" But he stopped himself, and edged out of sight into the shadows to survey the situation.

The giant mummy monster lay asleep on a slab of basalt rock, his ugly jaws partly open like those of a basking crocodile on a sandbank. He had the green head and saw-teeth of a crocodile, and the mummified body of a giant. His body and limbs looked like peeling tree-trunks, their bandages trailing over the edges of the stone. At his waist gleamed a set of bronze keys on a ring.

Josh swallowed drily at the thought of going near the monster.

He crept forward, hoping that the creature did not have supernatural powers that warned him of danger. The smell of the beast hit his nostrils like a wave as he drew close.

He measured the distance between himself and the

keys. They were big keys. Even if he managed to get them, they would be awkward to use. They were likely to scrape in the lock of the dungeon door. Perhaps the lock was rusty and would squeak. Once awakened, the monster would reach him in a few bounds. Josh needed to find a way to slow him down. He looked around for a length of cord or rope, but nothing useful met his eye.

He turned his attention to the mummy monster's vast, bandaged feet. The peeling bandages gave him an idea.

He edged closer and gently took one of the coarse trailing bandages in his fingers. He reached for another and joined the two ends together, knotting them. The monster's legs were huge. It would take more than one knot to trip him. Josh tied another two bandages. The mummy monster stirred, gurgled from the squelchy depths of a crocodile dream. Josh waited. The rumbling breathing steadied.

He tied another two loose ends of bandage together.

Now for the keys.

Then he heard a muffled cry.

Amy had clamped her hand over Harry's mouth. Harry's eyes were popping in excitement. They'd seen him. Josh put a finger to his lips. Amy nodded, understanding, and removed her hand from Harry's mouth.

Josh reached for the keys at the mummy monster's waist. Better take them with both hands to prevent them from clinking together. He felt as though he were breathing as loudly as the mummy monster. In his mind he saw the giant spinning round in a blur, the bandaged hands seizing his wrists.

Josh's fingers met the coldness of the bronze keys. Carefully he unhooked them from the monster's belt, holding them apart to prevent them from rattling together, and drew them away.

The mummy monster twitched. He moved his feet, spreading them apart, drawing the tied bandages taut at his ankles. Could he feel that he was bound?

Josh couldn't risk delaying. He tiptoed to the dungeon doorway and slid the key into the keyhole.

"Josh! Hurry!"

Amy's cry paralysed him.

"Behind you!" Harry yelled. For the first time he sounded mortally afraid.

Josh turned around. A great chunk of shadow had lifted from the slab of stone and was sliding off the edge. Crocodile head!

The mummy monster gave a bellow of anger that made Josh's eardrums cringe. The crocodile jaws were open to attack. The bulgy crocodile eyes directed slit-stares of hate at him.

Josh rattled the key in the lock. It wouldn't turn. *Wrong key*. He whipped it out and jammed in the other key.

"Josh—quickly!"

The mummy monster bulked like a mountain over Josh, and took a step towards him. Then the tied bandages drew tight. The monster tottered, flailed his arms in the air and crashed to the stone floor like a falling building.

Josh turned the key and threw open the door.

"Follow me—run!"

Amy and Harry bounded out of the chamber and up the stairs, Amy clutching Spy in her arms.

"You came for us!" Amy said as she ran. "I knew you would, Josh. I believed in you!"

"So did I!" Harry said. "But I was frightened silly! Good trick with the bandages!"

"We're not out of this yet," Josh said. "Keep running!"

The three fled along a passage, expecting at any second to hear the pile-driving thud of the mummy monster's footsteps in pursuit.

Josh slowed them before they reached the pit. The rope was still waiting where he had left it, jammed into a crack, and his skateboard was on the far side.

"I'll go over first," he said, "so I can catch you. Give me Spy." He undid his shirt buttons, tucked the cat safely inside his shirt and did up the buttons. Spy was warm, and his fur tickled Josh's stomach. "I'll take care of him, Amy, don't worry. We're not going to lose him a second time, I promise you!"

Josh swung across the pit to the other side. Amy went next, and then Harry. They were getting good at it.

But if they could swing across, so could the monster. When Harry landed safely on the other side, Josh kept hold of the rope.

"We've got to stop the mummy monster from following us," he said. "Let's cut the rope. Look for a sharp flake of stone."

Harry dug into his trouser pocket. "No need. My mum says you should never travel without your expeditionary gear." He produced a tiny pocket-knife and handed it over. Josh opened the blade and sawed at the rope. He cut it about half way through, then let it swing out over the void. "Let's get rid of old crocodile head once and for all," he said.

A bellow of rage announced the arrival of their pursuer. The mummy monster had reached the edge of the chasm!

"Yah! You can't reach us!" Harry baited it, regaining some of his earlier courage.

The monster snapped his scaly jaws in resentment and made a dive for the rope.

Josh waited for the creature to drop into the pit, but his own hopes took a tumble instead.

The rope should have broken, but it hadn't. It was holding!

"Run!" Harry said in terror.

The mummy monster sailed towards them. But he hadn't swung out far enough and couldn't reach the edge. Gathering momentum, he went back in a long pendulum arc. His crocodile jaws hungrily open, he began to return.

Harry and Amy were already starting to make a run for it, but Josh was unable to move. He couldn't believe what was happening. "I should have just kept the rope on this side, or cut it right through," he muttered. "But no, I had to get tricky and slice it only half way through. Stupid mistake."

"Come, Josh!" Amy called.

This is my fault, Josh told himself. *I'll stay here and face the mummy monster so the others can have a chance to escape.* A picture of the scorpion-filled passage flashed into his mind. Amy and Harry didn't know about that. Would they be able to get through it without him?

Amy ran back and pulled at his arm. "Come *on*, Josh!"

"Run, Amy," Josh said. "Go with Harry!"

"You can't fight the monster on your own!" Harry shouted.

It was too late to run. Crocodile head was swinging towards them, his bandages fluttering, the slit pupils of his eyes fixed on Josh.

"Please, Josh!" Amy was crying.

Josh broke free of Amy and stood waiting.

Half way across the void, the monster's jaws snapped shut in surprise as he found himself holding the frayed end of a useless piece of rope. He made a grab for the rest of it and caught a few strands in his fingers, but it slowed him for only an instant.

He fell with a scream into the void.

It was the thought of the scorpions in the last section that bothered Josh.

"We're going to need this," he said, picking up his board.

"You came here on a skateboard!" Harry exclaimed. "What use is a skateboard?"

When Josh told them about the armies of scorpions, Amy made a face. "We could take one of the other tunnels."

"I wouldn't advise it. There are pharaoh phantoms in those passages. You can hear them. Listen."

In the silence that followed, Josh waited for the sound that would announce the approach of the pharaoh phantoms. There it was. The shuffling started like a whisper and grew in the surrounding tunnels.

"Let's run!"

The floor led them gently upwards, and they stopped near the crest. The sea of scorpions was waiting for them on the last downward slope.

"Ooh, yuk! Gross!" Amy said. "How are we going to get through them?"

"We'll all use the skateboard. This could be tricky," Josh said, "but it's our only chance. I want you both to climb on the skateboard with me and stand as still as you can. We're going to ride the board together. It's wide enough and strong enough, provided you're steady and lean a bit when I lean. There's a slope coming up, so if we're lucky we can coast through the scorpions. Don't put your foot down, whatever you do!"

Harry looked scared. "Do you think we can all fit on? I've never been on a skateboard before!" He climbed on the back of the board. Amy went in front of him, her hands resting on Josh's shoulders. Harry held on to Amy's waist. Spy's head peeped out of Josh's collar.

"Let's go for a trial run," Josh said.

He put out his foot and gently pushed the board towards the slope. Amy swayed and clutched at his shoulders, and a ripple of unsteadiness went back to Harry, but they all stayed on board.

They were at the crest. Now the floor sloped away.

The scuttling scorpions filled the passage. The light of the wall lamps reflected on their bodies like moonlight on wavelets.

"Ready? Hold on, here goes!"

Josh launched the board with a long, steady push along the stone floor. The wheels and bearings complained under the children's combined weight, but they were on their way.

"Stay in the centre, or we'll tip over," Josh warned them.

They rolled towards the wave of scorpions, gathering speed.

A breeze hit Josh's face. He felt Amy's fingers tighten on his shoulders.

The skateboard with three children and a cat on it hurtled down the passage.

The first scorpion crunched and popped under a wheel.

"Ooer!" Amy shuddered.

Then another.

Crunch!

The wave parted.

"Mind your feet," Josh called to the others.

The scorpions lunged at their wheeled attacker, drumming their poison barbs under the deck of the skateboard.

Josh hoped the wheels would keep turning, willed them not to jam up with bits of squashed scorpions.

The scorpions scuttled and squeaked as the board ran through them. The wheels hit a fat scorpion and the board lifted. Harry almost came off. He clutched at Amy, and Amy grabbed at Josh to steady herself. Josh shifted his weight to correct the sway. It took all his powers of balance to hold them on course and keep them on the board as they ran out through the last wave and trundled along the corridor.

Clear of the scorpions, Josh put out his foot and gave one more hard push. They coasted to the black doorway of eternity.

After the narrowness and darkness of the corridor, the light in the museum exploded around them like a scene illuminated by flashlight. They spilled on to the floor of the Egyptian room.

They were back. They were safe.

They had left nightmares and mummy monsters behind.

Josh heard the shuffle of footsteps. A group of school-children was filing into the room. Then he saw the upright figure of Mrs Matheson. It was his class! *Today was the day of their school excursion!*

"You two go home," Josh whispered, taking Spy out of his shirt and handing him to Amy. "I have to stay. See you later."

Josh stood in front of a display case with his skateboard tucked under his arm.

"I see you're ahead of us all, Josh," Mrs Matheson said sharply. "You're so eager you scooted here on your skate-board. Seeing you're such a keen student of Egyptology, suppose you explain to the class about mummies and Egyptian funerary beliefs."

It was the last thing he wanted to do.

"We're waiting," Mrs Matheson said.

The Egyptian room seemed to sit up and listen. Josh looked from the empty stares of the painted eyes on the coffins to the laughing eyes of his classmates. He could imagine what they were thinking: *This is going to be good. Josh Wilson knows nothing about ancient Egypt. Josh only knows about computer games and skateboards.*

I'll show them, all of them, Josh thought, sudden anger flaring inside him.

"All right, listen," he said to the smirking class in a voice filled with authority. He knew what he was going to say: the words came easily into his mind, as if he was reading the boxes that had appeared on the screen in the Mummy Monster Game.

"The ancient Egyptians believed in an afterlife. They believed that in order to survive in the next world, the dead body must be preserved. To do this they made mummies. The body was steeped for seventy days in dry natron, during which process it lost seventy-five per cent of its body weight, and it was then wrapped in hundreds of metres of bandages. In the bandages were wrapped sacred amulets. The most important of all these was the scarab beetle, representing the heart, because the heart was believed to be the seat of the soul. The mummy had to have a house of eternity—a tomb and a coffin. These were not memorials, but eternity machines.

"When the souls of the dead reached the Egyptian heaven they were judged by Osiris. Osiris was a man-god who suffered, died and was resurrected to assure all Egyptians of immortality and to be the judge of their souls ..."

The class had gone very quiet.

"I'm impressed," Mrs Matheson said. She looked at Josh as if she had never really noticed him before.

"It's all in my essay," Josh said.

"I can hardly wait to read it," Mrs Matheson said. "Well done. Now, let's move on to the Art of the Potter display, class."

The class moved past Josh, breaking around him like water around a rock and staring at him with surprise. Josh followed, a smile on his face.

He'd won.

He'd rescued Amy, Harry and Spy, and he'd defeated the mummy monster. He felt good.

19

Real Life

The next day, after school, Josh sat at his desk in his bedroom and put down his pen. He had just finished writing his essay about the mythological beliefs of the ancient Egyptians.

It was twenty-one pages long.

His views about the Egyptians had changed since he'd played the Mummy Monster Game. He had believed that only ignorant people could worship a bunch of strange creatures with human bodies and the heads of apes, dogs, baboons, crocodiles and jackals. Only a primitive race could believe in a mummy king who would suffer and be torn to pieces only to be resurrected as the king of the underworld.

Now he wondered if these ideas went deeper.

He recalled what the game had said. In his mind he heard Harry reading the words once more:

IN EGYPTIAN MYTHOLOGY, OSIRIS WAS A MAN-GOD WHO SUFFERED AND DIED AND ROSE AGAIN TO REIGN ETERNALLY AS THE LORD OF THE AFTERWORLD AND THE JUDGE OF SOULS. THE MYTH OF THE RESURRECTION OF OSIRIS WAS A

Were the Egyptian beliefs to be taken literally, to be regarded as nonsense? Or were they attempts to grapple with deeper ideas? Did the ancient Egyptians really believe in animal-headed creatures, or were they expressing ideas about their universe in ways that people of their time understood?

Josh rewarded himself for finishing the essay with a skateboard ride around the block.

He saw the new boy paddling along the pavement on his board. The boy saw him coming and started to go faster.

"Hey, don't race off," Josh called to him.

"You want a fair start?"

"No, I don't want to race at all. Let's skate along together."

"You don't want to race me?"

"Nah." *People aren't simply things to compete against in games*, Josh reminded himself. *People are worth fighting for.* He hoped he'd never forget that.

The new boy smiled.

Later Josh returned the Mummy Monster Game in its box to Harry.

"Thanks, Harry, that was quite a game. But I think I've had enough of computer games for a while."

"Yes, thanks, Harry," Amy agreed. "It was a scary

game, but it did teach us things."

"You were very good, Amy," Harry said. "You saved us a few times. And Josh, you were great, and not just in the game."

"Thanks," Josh said.

Amy did have her turn on the computer, and she wrote a play for her school drama project.

Amy's play was about a brother and sister and their cousin—a brother who lost himself in computer games, a sister who spent all her time doing brilliant projects but never getting any praise for them, and a daredevil younger cousin who had thought the world was safe until one day he learned the wisdom of being a little afraid. The three children in her story played an imaginary Egyptian computer game with mummy monsters that came to life and filled their lives with terror.

The play was staged in the new term, after Harry had rejoined his mother, now back from Egypt. It was performed by members of Amy's class before an audience of schoolchildren, parents, family, and friends. Josh had supported Amy in insisting that their mother take time off work to attend the performance.

The parents in the audience were a bit stunned by the show, but the schoolchildren loved it and burst into wild cheers.

"Well, what did you think, Mum?" Amy said, running to meet her afterwards.

Her mother put her arms around Amy and hugged her. "I think your play was wonderful. I think I've been missing something very important and I'm sorry. And

I think I've been a bit of a mummy monster myself just lately."

Amy hugged her back. "Don't say that, Mum."

Josh smiled. *Mummy monster*. It was one of those plays on words that the ancient Egyptians would have loved.